Jake Couldn't Help It.

He'd run into Rain's house to get away from the approaching storm, but seeing her in the filmy outfit she was wearing, he found himself inspecting the way the wind pressed her wispy gown across her breasts.

"I had no idea the storm had gotten this bad," Rain said.

Feeling his body stirring, Jake thought about how bad it could get. Taking hold of her arms, he urged her back from the door. "You shouldn't stand so close," he said, schooling his voice to hide his lascivious fantasies.

"Um, in cases like this, you're always told to go to the most secure part of the house."

The hallway held promise. Jake could visualize himself backing her against a wall and kissing her until, weak-kneed, she would cling to him. But once given its lead, his imagination turned relentless. "They say a closet is better...."

Dear Reader,

Check out the hot hunks on the covers of this month's Desire books. These are our RED, WHITE AND BLUE heroes, and they sure are something, aren't they? These guys are red-blooded, white-knight, blue-collar types, and they're guaranteed to make the hot summer nights even *hotter!*

Next month, we have a new title from Diana Palmer that I know you'll all enjoy. It's called *Night of Love,* and as an extra bonus it's *also* August's *Man of the Month* title. Also coming up in August are titles from Dixie Browning, Lass Small, Linda Turner, Barbara McCauley and Cathie Linz. Don't miss a single one.

And I'm still waiting for answers to last month's questions. What exactly do you like in Desire? Is there anything we can do differently? Do more of? *Less* of? No answer is too outrageous!

So, until next month, enjoy! And don't forget to let me know how you feel.

Lucia Macro
Senior Editor

HELEN R. MYERS

JAKE

SILHOUETTE *Desire*

Published by Silhouette Books New York

America's Publisher of Contemporary Romance

SILHOUETTE BOOKS
300 East 42nd St., New York, N.Y. 10017

JAKE

Copyright © 1993 by Helen R. Myers

ISBN: 0-373-05797-0

First Silhouette Books printing July 1993

Printed in the U.S.A.

Books by Helen R. Myers

Silhouette Desire

Partners for Life #370
Smooth Operator #454
That Fontaine Woman! #471
The Pirate O'Keefe #506
Kiss Me Kate #570
After You #599
When Gabriel Called #650
Navarrone #738
Jake #797

Silhouette Romance

Donovan's Mermaid #557
Someone To Watch Over Me #643
Confidentially Yours #677
Invitation to a Wedding #737
A Fine Arrangement #776
Through My Eyes #814
Three Little Chaperones #861
Forbidden Passion #908

Silhouette Shadows

Night Mist #6

Silhouette Books

Silhouette Shadows Short Story Collection 1992
"Seawitch"

HELEN R. MYERS

satisfies her preference for a reclusive life-style by living deep in the Piney Woods of East Texas with her husband, Robert, and—because they were there first—the various species of four-legged and winged creatures that wander throughout their ranch. To write has been her lifelong dream, and to bring a slightly different flavor to each book is an ongoing ambition.

One

She stood before the closet-door mirror and stared at her reflection, determined to see the real Rain Neelson, determined to understand once and for all why Gilbert Wakefield had abandoned her for Polly Hansen. What crushed her was discovering how easy it was this morning. All she'd had to do was stop looking through the proverbial rose-colored glasses she'd been hiding behind for most of their relationship.

Yesterday's view had been better, she thought with a sniff as she eyed the ravaged figure before her. Twenty-four hours ago she'd still been Gil's fiancée and she'd felt...maybe not blushing-bride giddy, but settled. Of course, then her only problem had been worrying over finding decent salad tomatoes to go with the plump hen she'd been planning for dinner. When one plotted a coup, attention to details could prove the difference between

success and failure, and she'd definitely had a revolution
in mind for her and Gil.

Yesterday had been the day she'd finally found the
courage to push him beyond those gentlemanlike kisses
he'd been routinely bestowing on her since they were
seniors at Stiles Jr.-Sr. High School. She'd convinced
herself to seduce him into making love to her; by noon,
however, those fanciful aspirations had been replaced by
the shocking news that he'd run off with her best friend.
And, as though that humiliation wasn't enough, it turned
out she was the last person in Stiles, Mississippi to find
out!

Rain intended never to forget that last slap in the face.
The revelation might have been tolerable if the deceitful
couple had chosen a direct, prompt way of telling her.
Instead they'd left a note in the top drawer of the desk in
her office, a drawer she rarely opened more than a slit
when she needed her master keys for the post office. Polly
had known that, and it had been Polly who'd stopped by
yesterday morning and asked to borrow her phone sitting on that very desk.

How gullible of her to never have guessed a thing when
it should have struck her as odd. After all, Polly worked
directly across from the post office at the Main Street
Café; she could have used *their* phone. Well, she had her
answer now: her friend—*ex*-friend—was far more in-
genious and conniving than Rain had given her credit for.
That dizzy and capricious personality of Polly's had been
all pretense!

Yes, one day made a huge difference. *Face it,* she ordered herself, *you're not much to look at and you never
will be.* She stared at her nondescript brown hair and
pallid complexion, noting how washed out she looked.
Tired, too. Older than her twenty-nine years. There were

shadows under her eyes, a droop to her lips ... all creating an aura of defeatism.

Only the lingering droplets of water from her shower appeared unchanged. They slipped down over her shoulders and chest and trickled into the shallow valley of her breasts looking like liquid diamonds, beautiful in a way she would never be beautiful. They spilled over the front clasp of her bra and were absorbed by her plain nylon slip that the heat already had clinging to her midriff and thighs like a second skin.

How many times had she stood this way and pretended those ministreams of water were actually a lover's fingers playfully skimming—no, caressing her? She found it impossible to imagine such things now under the scorn of her bloodshot gaze, or to dare fantasize having the kind of face that could be heralded as inspiring. It would take closing her eyes to block all signs of grief and humiliation before she could pretend she was someone other than unexciting, skinny Rain Neelson, the oldest living virgin in Stiles; the woman—no, not even that—the *female* who'd failed to entice her own betrothed into an early celebration of their wedding night.

A sob caught in her throat. She pressed her fingers to her lips and shut her eyes against life's harsh reality. She was tired of hurting, and of focusing on all the reasons why she was miserable. For the better part of each day she lived with the fact that she would never be as intriguing as her name made her sound, never as vibrant and attractive as someone like Polly, nor as sensual and desirable as she yearned to be. She couldn't take it anymore.

She shut her eyes tight and dreamed of how it would be to climb out of her rut. She yearned for that brief, whimsical escape like never before.

It was those long pent-up needs and her utter loneliness that had her sliding her fingers from her lips down over her chin. She let her head drop back, traced the arching length of her throat until she came to the shallow dip where her pulse throbbed and moisture pooled. Dampening three fingertips there, she resumed her journey, following the escaping droplets of water.

Imagine. Behind her closed lids she envisioned herself as curvaceous instead of skinny, and pretended that three fingers had to journey in single file to pass between her breasts. They reached the border of her slip—lace in her mind's eye, not plain, unadorned nylon. There had been dozens of times when she'd willed Gil's lips to follow the same path. Of course, it had never happened. He'd always insisted he was too respectful of her to treat her like "a tramp." Ah, the benefits of hindsight: disrespectful her foot; he simply hadn't wanted her.

Don't think about him.

Fantasizing about a mystery lover was better. She'd been doing so for a while now. Born in the darkest corners of her dreams, through practice she'd learned to make him step out of those shadows at will. He wasn't timid, nor frustratingly polite…and he never stopped at the lace.

She let her fingers, *his fingers,* wander downward to her flat, firm abdomen. Her dream lover liked to sink to his knees and use his whole face to explore that smooth taut plain. He was at once tender, yet amorous and sexy. He never failed to whisper exciting, outrageous things, like how, next to her legs, he enjoyed lingering over this part of her anatomy best, exploring her sleekness, her womanliness.

But despite her efforts, she couldn't summon his whispery, gruff voice this morning. Still, the mere thought of him made her body come alive. Her nipples grew painfully hard. Hot pinpricks of awareness and excitement shot like fire-tipped arrows from her stomach downward, igniting a fever. Within seconds her legs were trembling. She used both hands to massage her thighs and ease their shaking, her aching.

Then somebody coughed.

It was a low, wheezing cough, and her immediate thought was that anything, even a bucket of ice water over her head, would have been preferable to hearing that horrible, humiliating sound.

Mortified, she spun around and saw the man standing on the other side of her screened front door. How stupid, stupid, stupid! she chastised herself. She should never have opened the hardwood door, never mind believing it often improved the airflow in her unairconditioned house.

Somehow her brain shifted to remote control. Somehow she snatched up the powder blue shirtwaist dress from her bed and dashed behind the privacy of a wall. "Who—who are you?" she demanded, amazed she could speak at all. "What do you want?"

"The name's Marlowe, ma'am. Jake Marlowe. Sorry for scaring you, but I was wondering if you knew when the station opened?"

"Station?"

"The gas station? Across the street?" he added, when several seconds passed and she failed to answer. "I picked up a nail outside of town and my bike's got a flat."

While he explained, she worked desperately to slip into her dress. Unfortunately, her fingers were shaking worse than her legs and she ended up having to go back and redo two buttons. She thought it a miracle that her jerky movements didn't snap them off.

Oh, Lord...he had to have seen everything. How many times had she warned herself to be careful? Granted, Stiles was a middle-of-nowhere town, and the shrubbery out front did create a privacy wall of sorts; but not for someone standing on the front stoop! She'd made an exhibition of herself. Her—the postmistress of Stiles! How could she face him?

She had to make him leave. No way could she bear coming out from her hiding place. It wasn't enough that Gil and Polly had destroyed her reputation, now this...this biker person was going to finish making her the laughingstock of the entire area, and all because of that eyesore across the street. It belonged to Angus England and everyone knew Angus was the town's biggest gossip.

"Ma'am?"

Drat his stubborn hide. He was too persistent she concluded with growing misery. No doubt he would stay rooted until she made an appearance.

With a vicious tug, which secured the belt in its farthest hole, Rain fought against the wave of exhaustion and nausea threatening to overcome her. What choice did she have but to go out there? she asked herself. She only wished there was time to slip into her panty hose and pumps first.

Barefoot, she stalked through the drapery-shaded living room, scowling at the man before her. She tried not to worry about not being able to see his face clearly, especially when his size suggested he was going to be as difficult to dismiss as he'd sounded.

From his wind-tossed hair—badly in need of a haircut—down his long, lean length to the faded jeans partially tucked inside cowboy boots, he evoked an earthy sensuality and an even greater elemental confidence that she found unsettling. No, not confidence, she corrected, not quite brave enough to give a disparaging sniff to his sweat-dampened T-shirt. Negligence.

But what bothered her most, when she got close enough to see, was the twinkle in his eyes and the way their mischievousness was compounded by his shark-toothed smile. Clearly, he'd seen as much as she feared, and he wasn't going to pretend otherwise. Whatever else he was, the man had the sensitivity and discretion of a lecher. She didn't like him one bit.

He liked her face…almost as much as he approved of everything else he'd seen. It surprised him because she'd obviously been crying.

Jake narrowed his eyes as the woman he'd been watching stepped through the inviting shadows of the living room to where daylight lit her fine-boned features. Yes, her face appealed to him for its quiet, un-pampered quality, which was in direct conflict with the fiery turbulence flashing in her eyes. Similarly, her abrupt self-consciousness seemed at odds with the graceful performance he'd witnessed before announcing himself.

When he'd first peered inside the aging but sturdy brick house, the sight of her standing there in her slip and not much else, while indulging in a sensual exploration of her body, had driven the breath out of him as though he'd taken a blow to the belly. He'd been tempted to remain silent, an apprentice voyeur quickly learning to relish sight's powerfully erotic effect on the senses.

Now she was covered from throat to calf, not unlike the prim schoolmarms he remembered from back in his school days. The sight annoyed him as much as it amused him, until he reconsidered her red-rimmed eyes and tear-ravaged face. Why had she been crying? Was someone else in the house? What if she was married and her old man found out he'd been standing there getting all hot and bothered over his wife?

"Mr. . . .Marlowe did you say?"

As she reached up to draw together her already buttoned collar, he saw she wore no ring on her left hand. "Yeah." He exhaled, relaxing somewhat. "But Jake will do."

"Mr. Marlowe. Isn't it customary where you're from to introduce yourself upon arriving on someone's doorstep?"

Lord, she had a voice. Southern mellow, it would have epitomized brown sugar and butter melting over a pecan roll—if she wasn't so riled. "I rang the doorbell."

"It doesn't work."

"That's why I announced myself the other way."

"After allowing yourself an eyeful."

He could have argued the "ful" part. As far as he was concerned, he was nowhere near finished with studying her.

Although she wasn't magazine pretty, he figured that when you were rawboned and weather roughened as he was, you didn't have a whole lot of room to hold a magnifying glass too closely to others. As far as he was concerned, she would do fine either way. Besides, artificially enhanced prettiness often faded with time. This woman, whom he judged to be in her mid-to-late twenties, would probably look much the same at fifty or sixty as she did now. Especially her small, firm breasts. Those breasts were the only reason he'd cleared his throat. Once he'd felt himself getting aroused, he'd reminded himself of how awkward things could get if the condition had become . . . overt.

On the other hand, he didn't feel she should get off scot-free, either. She ought to be more careful. A woman, especially one living on the outskirts of a town like this, never knew what type of characters were hanging around.

He tilted his head and asked, "Who're you madder at? Me for looking or you for forgetting the door was open?"

"Well, I never!"

It wouldn't surprise him if that was true. There was an untouched something about her, a stiffness crying out "repressed"... or could she be a virgin? Common sense told him he was nuts to guess the latter in this day and age. As rural as this town might be, she was old enough to have been around.

But as she fussed with her matronly hairdo, a twisted and coiled concoction held in place with combs and hairpins, he wondered if it was caution or fickleness that made her so uptight. The ice currently glinting in her crystal blue eyes—yes, he thought with satisfaction, they were blue—hid the sensuality and passion he'd witnessed before. Maybe she just hadn't met the right man to set it completely free yet.

A smile kept tugging at his mouth and he gave up trying to fight it.

"What's so funny?" she demanded.

"You don't want to know."

"Are you being insolent, Mr. Marlowe?"

"Only a bit," he admitted with a soft chuckle. "You happen to remind me of a school teacher I had in the second grade. She didn't have much of a sense of humor, either."

"There's nothing wrong with my sense of humor. What's more, I'm fed up with people jumping to conclusions about me. You have no...oh. Oh, my goodness.''

Her eyes went wide, her gaze unfocused. To Jake's growing horror, her already pale skin took on a pasty, greenish cast and she wavered like a statue in an earthquake. Convinced she was about to topple over in a dead faint, he grabbed the doorknob and yanked. This was no time to worry about being accused of breaking and entering or assault, he told himself. If she fell and hurt herself, she might blame him for *not* coming to her aid.

Luckily the door's hook-style latch wasn't set. He lunged inside and grabbed her by her upper arms. ''Easy,'' he crooned when, despite buckling knees, she weakly tried to push him away.

''W-what are you doing?''

He'd witnessed enough fainting spells in his thirty-five years to recognize when someone was about to pass out on him. Deciding it would be easier, and safer, he swung her into his arms. ''Trying to save you from cracking your head open. Do you want to lay down on the couch or your bed?''

''I'm not...I don't...Mr. Marlowe!''

He ignored her slurred protests and headed for the bedroom since the couch looked about as user-friendly as a sardine can. Not that the woman in his arms needed much space. She was a small thing and weighed less than what he packed on the back of his bike. What disconcerted him was how his body reacted to the feel of holding her close. Prickly disposition aside, she was soft and she smelled so clean and feminine that she immediately made him aware of his superior size and strength, and that he hadn't had a decent shower in two days.

The scent of lily of the valley seduced him. He drew it in deep and recalled sweeter days, such as the first time—

the only time—he'd laid a girl down on a blanket of sun-warmed grass and made love because he hadn't had the patience to wait until they were somewhere more private. The bittersweet ache those memories spawned had him swearing under his breath.

"Relax, lady. Between your dress and whatever's beneath it, you'd wear out a man no matter what was on his mind," he growled, circling the full-size bed. "Beats me what for, too. Are you the only person in these parts not to notice Mississippi's in the middle of a heat wave?"

"I dress in the manner appropriate to my position," she replied stiffly. "And if you don't put me down this instant, I'll—"

"What? Scream?" Annoyed that she was taking this all the wrong way, Jake was tempted to drop her on her salmon print bedspread. Maybe he didn't look like anyone's knight in shining armor, but hell, no one had ever gotten hysterical at the sight of him, either.

As it was, when he did set her down, he neglected being as gentle as he could have been. "Fine. Go ahead. Maybe whoever shows up will be able to tell me what I want to know so I can get out of here."

With that he went to the bathroom he'd noticed off to the left of the bed and, snatching up a washcloth, wet it with tepid tap water. Then he returned to her side and proceeded to dab the cloth against her forehead and cheeks. He could tell the act surprised her as much as his impulsive speech had.

"I assure you, this isn't necessary."

"Then you're as foolish as you are oversensitive." He brushed away her intrusive hands. "Except for your red eyes and nose you're as white as these walls, which means you've either got one hclluva hangover or—"

"I have *not* been drinking."

"—or you've been crying half the night." He lifted his eyebrows, inviting a response.

"That's none of your business."

"In other words you have, and probably over a man. Honey, whoever he is, I'll bet you anything he's not worth it."

"You have to be the rudest, most brutish person I've ever met."

Jake considered her flashing eyes and the way she had her hands clenched into fists at each side of her hips. If he'd ever seen a woman who needed some tender loving care, this was the one. But he was the wrong man and this was definitely the wrong place. Not that he had any doubts about his ability to be kind; he'd merely decided long ago to mind his own business and not get too deeply involved with other people's troubles, especially when it came to heartache.

"Actually, I'm a real sweetheart," he replied, keeping his tone cheerful as he went to rinse the cloth again. When he returned, he sat down on the edge of the bed and repeated the process of bathing her face. "Of course, I've a gut hunch you don't believe that."

"Your gut is right."

Jake gave in to a low laugh before considering her more speculatively. Whoever she was, she wasn't the stereo-typical hothouse flower; she was fighting the hurt and pain she was feeling as much as her faintness, and he couldn't help but admire that. "Will you at least tell me your name?"

She shifted her gaze to the left of his elbow. "Rain Neelson."

"Pretty."

She shrugged and kept her eyes averted.

"You don't like it?"

"I like it very much. But I happen to believe it would suit someone else much better than it does me."

"I see." And he did. He just didn't agree. "It suits you a helluva lot more than, say, Ethel would."

She shot him a look that told him she held his opinion in about as much regard as she did his language. "Tell me, how many Rains do *you* know whose fiancé ran off with her best friend?" she snapped. "No, Mr. Marlowe, I have no illusions about myself."

So that was what all this prickliness was about. Jake felt a surge of empathy that was almost as disconcerting as the strange satisfaction he'd felt upon learning she wasn't married.

"When'd it happen?" he asked, his curiosity getting the better of him.

"Yesterday."

Which explained why she felt the way she did. She probably hadn't slept or eaten since. "Did you love him?"

"Of course, I did. I told you, he was my fiancé."

"When did that ever count for anything? People get married all the time to people they don't love."

Rain Neelson lifted her chin. Like her forehead and straight nose, it was sharply defined and alluded to a stubbornness he'd already recognized. "Men, maybe. But for women it's different."

"Is that a fact? Well, let me tell you something, lady, the woman I once planned to marry didn't think so. Otherwise she would never have found it quite so easy to seduce my brother once she'd learned he was the sole heir to the family ranch," Jake replied, before he had a chance to think about what he was admitting.

As Rain's tearstained eyes widened with surprise and curiosity, he mentally kicked himself. Where the devil had that come from? It wasn't his way to confide in strangers. He could pass the time of day with anyone, even share a meal with a person he'd stopped to help on the road. But to carry a fainting woman he would probably never see again to bed and confide his most personal, humiliating secret?

It had to be her, he decided with an inward sigh. That innocent and disturbingly honest face of hers had suckered him into it.

"I'm sorry," she murmured, grabbing at the slipping washcloth he'd abruptly released. She lowered her gaze to where he was rubbing his hands against his jeans, then looked away even faster. "The funny thing is, I'd have guessed you'd be the one to tempt a woman to go astray."

"Yeah, that's hilarious," Jake muttered, ready to change the subject. "What the heck, it was a long time ago."

"But if you loved her..."

"I said it doesn't matter!"

She recoiled as though he'd struck out at her, and that left him feeling farther away from knighthood than ever. He didn't mean to come off so uptight, but she had a knack for making him feel as edgy as he was obviously making her. Being in her bedroom was having its effect on him, too.

It had been a long time since he'd been around anything like this. Lately, when he did bother to seek a place out of the weather, the rooms he tended to find on back roads were at cheap hotels and derelict boardinghouses. There the curtains and bedspreads—when there were any—often looked as washed out as most of his clothes.

This room was clean and feminine and full of personal odds and ends. It again reminded him that he had no business being here, despite the urge he had to kick off his boots, stretch out beside her and sleep for a week.

"It's been so many years, I can't remember if I really did care or not," he finally admitted, adding an indifferent shrug.

"Did you know her a long time?"

"A few months. How about you and your...?"

"Since grade school."

"He the first guy you ever kissed?"

"The only one."

Since she'd gone back to avoiding his gaze, Jake focused on her mouth. Not his smartest move. She had nice lips... on the small side, and not too full... but sweet looking, made for forgiving smiles and tender laughs. He found himself wondering how she would taste. *Like new,* a gremlin in his gut taunted.

The thought began to gnaw. Soon it grew impossible, as bad as his yearning for breakfast. There would have to be something refreshing about kissing a woman who didn't make *him* feel like a novice, he concluded. Prompted by the relentless demon, he asked, "Did you like it?"

"It?"

"Kissing him."

Her lips parted. She began to moisten them with her tongue, seemed to realize where he was looking and instead sat up. "I think I'm feeling much better."

The same demon that had gotten him into this mine field of tension prompted Jake to stay put, which only served to bring them into closer proximity. "No need to get uptight," he cajoled, inspecting the tiny garnet in her equally small earlobe. "It's strictly a rhetorical question."

"Mr. Marlowe..." Rain began, and with obvious reluctance met his sardonic smile. "You're an incorrigible man and I can't believe I'm actually having this conversation with you, let alone allowing you into my house."

"Your bedroom, if you want to get melodramatic. But don't forget, you didn't exactly have a choice in the matter, so don't be too hard on yourself."

"My conscience thanks you, now will you please move? I'm feeling much better and I'm already late for work."

Jake didn't believe her, at least not the part about feeling better. Only a day of self-indulgence, decadently rich foods and ego stroking would cure what ailed her, but he wisely kept the theory to himself. Instead he challenged, "Answer my question first."

"Certainly not. However, I will tell you that Angus England should be arriving to open his garage at any moment. Why don't you go back across the street and wait for him?"

Jake couldn't help himself; he laughed briefly and tugged at his ear. "Does, um, that prim act work for most people around here?"

"This is not an act."

"No? A moment ago you were all soft and vulnerable and sympathetic. Downright appealing if you ask me. But I'm not too crazy about this side. A guy could get his feelings hurt if he thought you were being serious. I kinda like the way you stick out that chin, though. I'll bet once you set your mind to something, there's not much you back away from. Care to give it a try?"

Her owlish blink spoke of innocence and shyness, but Jake had to respect her for her great recovery. "I think I lost track of this conversation ten minutes ago," she replied coolly.

"Chicken. You know exactly what I mean." As she began to turn away, he shifted one hand under her chin to keep her still. "Why don't you kiss me and up your average?"

"Av...you're not serious?"

"Why not? Consider it an opportunity to find out if you're wasting saltwater over a guy who treated you like a throwaway towel. Who knows? I might be what the doctor ordered to chase away your blues."

"More likely a doctor would have you committed," she muttered, lowering her lashes.

It irked him to be deprived of her animated eyes. "You don't have to be scared...or embarrassed."

Her head shot up. The chill in her gaze dropped another ten degrees, delighting Jake.

"For your information," she sputtered, "I'm neither. But I warn you, Mr. Marlowe, I am getting angry."

"Even better." He grinned. "Only don't waste it or your passion. Come on, Miss Rain. Prove to yourself that your ex-fiancé was the one who made a mistake. You know you're tempted. I can see it burning like silver fire behind all that ice in your eyes. Do it."

It was crazy to flirt with trouble and who knew what else. He acknowledged that he deserved a swift kick in the butt, along with a police escort out of town. But before common sense could override his inexplicable impulses, Rain slid a hand behind his head, grabbed a handful of his hair and pressed her mouth to his.

Her aim was off and her lips were about as soft as a branding iron baked in lead, but once Jake recovered from the brief surprise that she'd actually called his bluff, all that was temporary and correctable. Angling his head, he centered their kiss, then he focused on showing her the difference between anger and passion.

Curiosity, he soon learned, was a dangerous thing. When he'd first started this nonsense, he'd done so out of some strange sense of compassion and frustration. He'd always hated like hell for people to burrow under rocks when life kicked them in the teeth—especially if they were made of stronger stuff, as he instinctively knew was the case with Miss Rain Neelson. But as he coaxed her lips into softening against his, to mimic the slow, rocking motion he was showing her, he felt a long-dormant hunger stir within him.

For the last few years he'd lived life with a brutal simplicity. Basic work, basic food and... Okay, he amended, maybe his existence hadn't been entirely deprived. But he traveled when and where impulse took him, never staying long enough to get attached to anything or anyone. He put in an honest day's labor for whoever his employer was at the moment, and enjoyed himself through it all. He'd intended this kiss to be an extension of that easygoing pattern, but he should have known better.

Rain Neelson was a woman who'd been craving attention for a long time, and she was a quick study. Jake patiently parted her lips with his own. Her anger melted into hesitancy, then desire as his tongue teased and invited hers into a wicked duel. He could only guess what she was feeling; however, she soon had him forgetting the reason he'd instigated the kiss in the first place.

At the sound of her low moan, he shifted closer and wrapped his arms around her. The feel of her small, dancer's breasts tightening with need was as arousing as her increasingly aggressive response. He imagined how it would be to lay her back into the pillows, unbutton the prim shirtwaist dress she wore and explore her supple body. It only intensified his hunger and he sought satisfaction by showing her with his lips, then his tongue, what he would really like to be doing. That earned him a panicky whimper and an instant later she broke away to bury her face against his shoulder.

"Oh, my goodness," she breathed, her voice thin and shaky.

He had to swallow to find his own voice. "You can say that again."

It was reflective of his lifelong luck—or rather, the lack of any—that before either of them could say or do anything else, they heard the sound of footsteps on the front walk, followed by a rap at the door. "Rain? Yo! You know anything about that motorcycle parked at my place? Rain?"

Her withdrawal was immediate. Although Jake didn't attempt to stop her, he murmured, "It's okay."

"It is not!" she whispered back, her expression horror stricken. "That's Angus! What if he comes in?"

It was on the tip of his tongue to offer a dry quip, but seeing the frantic way she fussed with her hair and dress, he changed his mind and forced himself off the bed. His body didn't think that was such a good idea. There was nothing he could do about the obvious state of his arousal, but he ran his hands through his hair, trying to make it look presentable. "I'll go talk to him," he told her.

"Yes. No! I mean, don't you dare tell him anything about—"

"What do you take me for?" he shot back. One glance and he had all the illumination he needed. That stung because he had, after all, been trying to help her regain some of her confidence. "Hell. Far be it for me to be accused of tarnishing your sterling reputation," he growled under his breath. "Why don't I just crawl out your bathroom window and come around the front?"

"That's a wonderful idea." In her enthusiasm she all but pushed him to the tiny compartment.

Jake decided next time he had any harebrained ideas he would take a flying leap into the first river he came across. "Sure. Anything to please a lady," he grumbled, as he made short work of the screen. Flimsy thing would barely hold back a mosquito, he thought, his mood shifting from injured to uncharitable.

"Please hurry!"

Halfway through backing out the window, he scowled at her, but the moment he saw her apologetic wince, he forgave her. Who knows, he thought, maybe it wasn't her fault that she was too straitlaced and high-strung for her own good.

He dropped to the ground, torn between cursing and apologizing. "One more thing," he said, as between the two of them they got the screen back in place.

He ignored the louder "Rain?" from the front of the house.

So did she. "What?"

She mouthed the word rather than spoke it. He knew because his gaze was once again locked on her kiss-swollen lips.

"Yes?" she prompted, when he lost track of what he'd meant to say.

"For what it's worth, your ex-fiancé was a fool."

Two

Jake was still calling himself a softhearted jerk when he rounded the house and made his presence known to Angus England. But introductions were at the handshaking stage before he actually paid close attention to the aging giant before him.

Angus was wearing a cast on his right arm. It went from hand to shoulder and was held against his chest by an equally immaculate sling that emphasized the discoloration of bruised fingers. With a sympathetic shake of his head, Jake offered his left hand instead. "That looks new."

Angus snorted. "Plaster's barely dry." He gestured to the offending harness with disgust. "Got it by being stupid last night." They cut across Rain's meticulous but heat-suffering front lawn and the empty farm-to-market road. "Tried to put up a new TV antenna on my roof.

Turns out I could've stuck a broomstick in each ear and gotten better reception for all my trouble.''

Relieved that Angus's preoccupation with his injury kept him from asking questions about his sudden appearance from the back of Rain's house, Jake offered an understanding nod and grin. The old man was a character and it wasn't difficult to picture the comical sight he must have made with his big feet and long limbs trying to negotiate the rungs of a ladder. A respectable six feet himself, Jake gauged that the top of his head could easily fit under the old-timer's unshaven salt-and-pepper whiskers.

From his shaggy silver hair, partially hidden beneath a blue baseball cap, to his cowboy boots, Angus reminded him of an aging version of himself: lean as rawhide, tough skinned like beef jerky and speculative to the point his eyes were narrowed into a perpetual squint. If Jake didn't have sharp memories of his late tobacco-chewing, cattle-cussing father, he might have wondered whether his momma hadn't once engaged in an indiscretion. The one thing nullifying the whimsical theory was that his mother had lived and died never once traveling more than twenty miles from the ranch. Besides, a Marlowe never lost a woman he'd set his mind to having . . . unless it was to another Marlowe.

Angus came to a stop by one of the two gas pumps that were more rusty than red. He used a key from the collection hooked to a belt loop on his sagging jeans to unlock it and its twin. Afterward, he rested his good arm on top and uttered a belly-deep sigh. ''Damn, but it's gonna be another hot one.''

Jake grunted, seeing no reason to waste energy on the obvious. What also proved apparent was that Angus wasn't in a hurry to open up shop any sooner than necessary.

The combination service station and convenience store reminded him of many he'd come across in his travels, except that it was built more haphazardly. Cinder blocks, tin and whatever else Angus must have found after a tornado passed through the area or an eighteen-wheeler lost its load, created an architect's nightmare. But considering the number of empty soda bottles stacked in wood trays beside the two soft-drink machines and the shelves of merchandise Jake noticed beyond the plate-glass windows, cosmetics didn't seem to have a negative effect on business.

Beside the ramshackle building, the slightly tilting, white-and-green trailer—where he'd checked before going across the street—didn't appear in much better shape. Once again Jake eyed the flat on its front left side and experienced renewed doubts as to whether he would get his own tire repaired.

The rest of the town—or what he could see of it, because most was hidden behind a barn a few hundred yards down the road—seemed quaint and as tidy as Rain's place. Jake promised himself to drive through it before heading back toward the main highway.

"Guess cable TV hasn't made it out to this part of the country yet," he said, picking up their conversation where they'd left off.

"Heck, son, we only did get a zip code ten years ago. Gotta allow some time for adjusting. But we do believe in progress. Did you get to meet Rain over there?"

"Uh . . . for a second." Helpless not to, Jake recalled the scent of lily of the valley.

"She's our postmaster. Or I guess you'd have to call her a postmissus, I ain't one for formalities. A real lady she is, though. Takes after her mother in that department. Course, her ma was the looker in the family. Still, Rain's got the breeding. Always makes me feel I should wash my hands before I put gas in her car, know what I mean? There she goes now. Guess she's running late today."

Slightly annoyed at the man's narrow-minded commentary but unable to ignore his directive nod, Jake turned and spotted Rain hurrying to a two-door compact, which had drawn him to her house in the first place. It was the same frosty blue of her eyes, the same cool shade of her dress. She was shoving on sunglasses and walked with her head ducked, like a celebrity trying to slip undetected past a reporter.

No doubt about it, the lady was a case. *But not yours.* He would do well to remember that and get past whatever it was about her that drew him and roused his protective instincts.

Common sense aside, he couldn't help but note how her face looked pinched again, her body tense. He could tell his parting words to her were already forgotten. Maybe the kiss, too. Reality had reclaimed its hold on her and was turning her back into acting like an ugly duckling hiding behind haughtiness.

There was no denying his curiosity about what was going on in her head. Too bad he couldn't attach her to a lie-detector machine and get at the truth.

"Rain Neelson, did you enjoy kissing Jake Marlowe? You do admit you kissed him back, don't you? Will you admit you got as caught up in it as he did? Are you curious to know if..."

He gave himself a mental shake. "Doesn't look too cheerful, does she?"

"She had a tough blow yesterday. The news is all over town."

Jake remained silent, having heard all he wanted to about that. Apparently, so had Rain because when she sped by, she pretended to have something in her eye and ignored Angus's wave.

"Yep," Angus drawled, seemingly unaffected. "That's what's ailing her all right."

Without being asked, the old-timer rattled off his version of Rain's humiliation. Despite his lack of tact, he proved more sympathetic than Jake had originally judged him.

"You sound as though you've known her a long time," he said, once the man paused to scratch at a mosquito bite on his uninjured arm.

"Well, you might say she grew up under my nose, except that her mama kept her inside a lot. Miz Neelson had what women around here used to call a 'fragile' constitution. With Bert—that was Mr. Neelson—traveling so much, I suppose she used Rain to ward off her loneliness." Having satisfied one itch, Angus struggled to insert his index finger into his cast and scratch at another. "Yep. That's the way it goes."

"Guess so."

The uninspiring response earned Jake another look, this one somewhat disappointed. Clearly, Angus was in the mood to wax eloquent and expected proper encouragement. "Damn, but it's gonna be a hot one," he muttered, falling back on the reliable once the invitation failed to come. "You didn't bring along any rain from wherever it was you came from, did you?"

"Wish I could say I did."

"Don't believe I caught whereabouts you said you was from."

"Didn't say, but it's Texas."

"Whewie, there's a big spot of territory."

"A small town outside of Wichita Falls I haven't been back to in years," Jake confessed, aware there was no avoiding a few details.

Angus glanced at the motorcycle by the tin and plyboard garage doors. "Been traveling some?"

"When the mood strikes."

"Guess the time to do that's when you're young."

Not according to his mother. During his next-to-last call home, she'd pointed out that at thirty-three he wasn't a kid anymore; he should accept his family for the way they were, she'd said, and come home to help his brother on the ranch.

After relocating a month later he'd telephoned again and learned she was gone. She'd passed away the week before in her sleep.

"How much of a hurry are you in to get that flat fixed?" Angus asked, cradling his injured arm as though it were a baby. "Reason I'm asking is 'cause I don't know how much help I can be to you for a while."

Jake fought a cough and decided to pass on asking for a definition of what "a while" meant. "No problem. If you don't mind me using your tools, I can take care of it myself."

"That a fact? Well, good. But no sense rushing a sweat. C'mon inside and we'll set some by the fan, maybe have us a Coke. Never seen it so hot a body could get heatstroke from talking."

Had they been discussing her? Barely containing her anger and embarrassment, Rain gripped the steering wheel to keep her hands from shaking. She was almost certain they had been. Whoever said women were the worst gossips of the world hadn't spent any time around Angus England. And that Jake Marlowe person...

Had he told Angus about being in her bedroom? What if he described everything? How he'd stood at her front door and watched her touching herself? How she'd kissed him like a love-starved spinster?

With a gasp, she hit her brakes, but even so she nearly jumped the curb and made a new entryway into the back wall of the post office. Shaken, she shifted into Park and shut off the car's engine, but she didn't have the energy to get out right away and go inside. Not yet. In fact, the way things were going, she didn't know if she had the strength to live in Stiles any longer.

It had been crazy to fall prey to Jake Marlowe's teasing and prodding. Even recognizing it for what it was, she'd felt herself succumbing. Why now after all these years?

In grade school she'd managed to ignore the other girls who'd teased her because her hair was fine and straight and couldn't hold a curl like theirs. In junior high she'd survived the whispers and giggles at being the last girl in her gym class to trade in her undershirt for a bra. In her senior year she'd held her head high, struggling valiantly not to appear to mind that, under duress from his parents, Gil had taken his cousin to the senior prom and not her. She'd even been determined to hold on to her dignity until the furor died down over this latest upheaval with Gil and Polly. But Jake Marlowe was undermining her plans, maybe because in every other case she had been a victim, but this time she'd been a participant.

Memories came vividly, and she felt her face heat from a new rush of embarrassment. To actually have grabbed the man and kissed him, never mind that he'd provoked her. Then to try to argue with herself that she'd done it only in the hopes that it would make him go away! Oh, yes, she'd known what she'd been doing.

And once that valve of passion had been opened there'd been no shutting it off. What upset her most was learning how shockingly wonderful those few moments had been. If Angus hadn't arrived when he did, how far would they, would *she* have let things go? She touched her fingertips to her mouth, closed her eyes and moaned with renewed despair.

It wasn't fair to have the power to make someone feel such emotion. Until today lust had been a gray word to her. Jake Marlowe had advanced her education and made it very familiar, and desirable.

Never again would kissing be as simple as two pairs of lips touching together with warmth and affection the way it had been with Gil. Now she understood there could, there *should* be much more.

Even sitting here, she could still feel him teasing her lips with his tongue, the strange but exciting tingling shooting through her as he'd entered her mouth and touched her for the first time, the restlessness and fever spawned when he'd stroked her again and again....

"Hey! You're gonna roast alive in there."

The shout was accompanied by a brisk rapping on the hood of her car. With a silent groan, Rain focused on Norman Uttley, one of her two route drivers, peering at her through her windshield. She sent him a weak smile before snatching up her purse and climbing out of her vehicle.

"Morning, Norm," she said, grateful that he simply waved and continued toward his four-wheel-drive truck. A pleasant man with a grandfatherly countenance to match his Santa Claus physique, she sometimes wished she could clone him. Instead, she supervised a motley crew. Scarcely inside, she was reminded of that.

"The air conditioner stopped working at 5:52."

Rain didn't know why she expected any other kind of reception simply because her world had been turned upside down. She hadn't asked for pity or special treatment when she'd phoned in earlier and advised her second-in-command that she would be late. But she couldn't help wishing George Gibbons could take a little less pleasure in adding to her misery.

"Thank you, George. If it weren't for that news flash, I might never have figured out why I have the sudden urge to hyperventilate." She didn't care if she did sound like a woman suffering from a severe case of PMS, the conniving twerp had his nerve. It wasn't her fault that she'd been chosen to head the Stiles branch instead of him, but she was sick of him taking it out on her. "Why didn't you tell me this when I phoned?"

She watched him push his clear-framed glasses back up his nose and give her a tight-lipped smile, a smile no warmer than her current feelings toward Gil and Polly. "I felt you needed more time to get your emotional state under control. I don't know why you didn't take my advice and take the day off."

She would rather have stood up before her church congregation and declared she preferred rap music to hymns. "Thank you for your concern, George, and your selfless interest in getting the town's mail delivered regardless of personal sacrifice. But I couldn't bring myself to overload you like that."

His smile grew brittle. "You did anyway. Bud called in sick, too."

Bud Cox was their other route driver. He had a fondness for spending his paycheck on beer, billiards and blondes—although not in that particular order. Since yesterday had been payday, no doubt the overgrown adolescent was holed up with his latest infatuation, recuperating from one excess or another. That was hardly her fault; however, Rain knew what George was really driving at.

"I know you feel having the second highest seniority around here should release you from having to do rural route deliveries," she said, trying to remain diplomatic, "but you also know Malva's car isn't up to making that trip. You'll have to take Bud's route yourself."

"Being familiar with your fairness, I've already loaded. I was only waiting for you to get here because I didn't want to leave the place—" he glanced over his shoulder to where the final member of their group was rolling a bin of outgoing mail to the sorting table "—underattended."

Rain gripped the soft leather of her purse in an effort to restrain her impulse to retaliate. Of the many insults and biases she could and did tolerate, prejudice was not one of them. "And now I'm here," she replied, adding censure to her tone, "so by all means head on out. In the meantime, I'll call our electrician."

"Don't bother. I've already tried," he announced smugly, stretching his neck in a characteristic attempt to meet her at eye level. "He's booked. Everyone is. There's no hope of getting help until next week at the earliest."

He was enjoying this. As her stomach rolled threateningly, Rain brushed by him and went to her office. She was shaking with such anger she needed the distance from him. Better that, she fumed, than to give in to something she might regret later—such as stamping Return to Sender across his forehead.

Unfortunately, as stifling as the main sorting room was, her closet-size office was far worse. Within moments she could feel her antiperspirant failing her and the damp elastic of her bra beginning an itch she yearned to scratch. After shoving her purse into her bottom desk drawer, she released the top button of her dress and reached for the phone book.

At least the service counters were closed on Saturdays, she thought, her mood sinking further as a trickle of perspiration began running down her throat. If people thought she wasn't much to look at under normal circumstances, they would really have something to gossip about once she spent a few hours in this sauna.

She was hanging up on her third unsuccessful call when Malva Johnson scuffled in. As hot as she was, Rain felt a surge of sympathy for Malva. In her typical uniform of sleeveless tank top and stretch jeans, the heavyset woman's clothing appeared sprayed on her lush body.

"Here," Malva said, handing over a paper cup that turned out to be ice water. "I wrestled with Georgie for the last of the ice cubes before he left. Thought you could use this."

Amused by her irreverent wit, but not surprised at the shy kindness, Rain thanked her and took an eager sip. A loner from the day she'd been hired, Malva was the only other woman at the post office, yet she never involved herself with any of the friction that went on. But she did her job well and Rain had tried to respect her unspoken wish to simply be allowed to do a decent day's work for a decent day's pay.

"How was the load this morning?" she asked, stopping her from retreating farther out the door.

Malva glanced at her warily. "Light, even for a Saturday. We'll be outta here in another two hours."

"You will," Rain agreed, "but I have to find someone to repair that blessed air-conditioning unit and then
stay with him until the job's done. You wouldn't by any
chance know of a magician who free-lances as a guard-
ian angel?"

Cautious brown eyes considered her for a long, solemn moment. "You serious?"

Tempted to laugh hysterically and indulge in an acerbic retort, Rain settled for a nod. "You do, don't you?"

"Got a brother-in-law who's trying to make it on his
own."

"Why didn't you *say* something sooner?"

"You got a regular serviceman for this place. Besides," she added, lowering her voice although no one
remained in the building except the two of them, "I don't
like to cause no trouble where there's already enough."

Rain could have hugged her. "Never mind George.
He's just been moody lately. Do you think your brother-
in-law is available now?" Even then she sensed hesitation on Malva's part. "The job pays time-and-a-half and
if he has to run past five, it'll be double time, the same as
it would be for our regular serviceman."

"Okay." Finally hope lit Malva's somber gaze, and
gratitude widened her smile. "I'll call him for you."

Oz Davies had a great deal in common with his sister-
in-law, Rain thought as she drove home later that afternoon. Low-key and quiet, it was his diffidence that had
forced Rain to take matters into her own hands.

Once he'd discovered the problem with their system—
simply a matter of a burned-out switch and neglected
maintenance—she had been determined to reassure him
of how pleased she was with his honesty and his service.
It had seemed not only fair but good business sense to

immediately hire him as a replacement for the other electrician. Then she had asked him to take on the care of her unit at the house as well.

George, of course, would be critical when he found out, but Rain wasn't in the mood to worry about him. All she wanted was to get home and out of her wilted clothes. She fantasized about how nice it would be to draw a cool bath and soak the heat, tension and perspiration off herself for an hour or so. Maybe even have a glass of that sherry she kept in the back of the pantry for her once-a-year cold.

But due to the drought accompanying their heat wave, Stiles had been forced to adopt a strict water-rationing program. The best she could hope for would be a thirty-second rinse under the shower. First, she reminded herself, eyeing her car's fuel gauge, she needed to fill up the gas tank.

As she pulled into Angus's station and drove over the rubber hosing that sounded the bell above the door, she silently willed the old codger to behave himself once he came to greet her. She felt too drained to deal with his inquisitiveness.

But there was no sign of him. About convinced he'd gone home having forgotten to lock up, she saw the trailer door open and a man step out. It wasn't Angus.

"No!" she whispered, aghast. "It can't be."

She couldn't believe this was happening to her.

With long-legged, loose-hipped strides he crossed over to her, then bent at the waist to grin through the rolled down window. "Afternoon, Miss Rain. Fill 'er up?"

"What are you doing here?" she demanded, her voice not quite steady because her heart, her entire body was filling with dread.

"Working."

"No. No, you're supposed to be *gone*."

"Am I? Who said?"

She couldn't stand his grin any more than she could meet the wicked twinkle in his eyes. She scanned the area once again. "Where's Angus?"

"Gone home a long time ago. His arm's giving him heaps of trouble."

"And he left the place open like this?"

"Why not? I'm a responsible employee."

With that bombshell he moved to the back of her car and began unscrewing the tank cap behind the rear license plate. Rain twisted in her seat and poked her head out the window to stare after him. "Excuse me? You're going to work here?"

"That's right."

"Why?"

He flipped on the noisy pump. It sounded like her garbage disposal ever since she'd broken a jar of pickles in the sink and several chunks of glass had fallen into the system. "What?" he called back, his expression innocent.

Convinced he was being intentionally obtuse, Rain thrust open the car door but had to fight her seat belt before she could climb out. By the time she succeeded she'd knocked one of the combs loose from her hair. Feeling like a hag, she did her best to repair the damage, but not before another comb slipped and bounced onto the gas- and oil-stained cement.

Jake proved faster and crouched down, retrieving it. As he handed it back, his gaze swept over her coiffure. She had no idea what he could be thinking since his eyes were impenetrable slits despite the carport supplying a small square of shade. She could imagine, however, and although she would swear to anyone that she had no interest in the man, her ego didn't need to be reminded how both times they'd been together he'd seen her looking her worst.

"How long is it when it's not twisted and tortured like that?" he asked, his tone reflective.

She couldn't keep from touching her hair. "This is a style I picked up from a very popular fashion magazine."

"The same kind of magazine where the models look like they're wearing stuff I've seen on rodeo clowns?"

She refused to admit she agreed about some of the fashions, and worked at tucking strands into place. Under normal circumstances, it wouldn't have been a problem; she'd been wearing the style for so long she didn't need a mirror. But her intent audience was making her efforts totally inept.

"Want some help? Maybe I can show you what else I'm good at."

"No, thank you." Refusing to be won over by his idea of charm, she gave up and viciously stuck in the comb, not caring what the end result was. "Just answer my question, please."

"Anyone ever tell you how much the sun brings out the highlights in your hair? I always thought ash was a shade that had to come out of a bottle."

"I do not dye my—" Seeing the twitch of his wide thin lips, she uttered a wordless sound. "*Why* are you working here?"

"Why does anyone work anywhere? It was time to look for a job again, and I'm not one to turn my back on opportunity."

He made sense. In theory. Her problem was that his timing couldn't be worse. "Please don't take this the wrong way, but I'm not going to be comfortable with you staying in town."

"Why not?"

Her laugh held little humor. "You must be joking."

"Not when it comes to my livelihood. Or giving my word."

"That's very admirable, I'm sure, but the fact remains your presence in town is going to be awkward for me. Under the circumstances, I could do without being the source of any additional gossip."

"What do I have to do with that?"

"Really! Do you think I didn't see you and Angus chattering away like two hens this morning?"

"Actually, the way your nose was stuck in the air, I found it amazing you could even see to steer."

The pump shut off. Jake removed the nozzle and replaced it in its slot. Then he turned back to the car and screwed the cap in place.

"If you're worrying whether or not I told Angus about what happened at your place this morning," he continued, "you can relax. He was so busy talking, he didn't have time to ask. But if he had," he added, rounding to her side and sandwiching her between him and the car, "I'm not the kind to kiss and tell, know what I mean?"

The hot metal of the small sedan seeped through her clothing, heating her bottom and the backs of her thighs. But it was no more intense than the searing embarrassment scorching Rain on the inside. "The problem is I only have your word, which is small comfort," she replied, her throat parched like the sun-scorched fields around them.

"Then you'll have to wait and see, won't you?"

Wait? She couldn't afford to, she thought, finding it equally uncomfortable to focus on his chest. His dirt-smudged T-shirt stretched across his taut muscles, almost like a second skin, definitely a blatant exhibition of his fitness.

She found relief in watching the placard swinging from the center post that advised motorists to shut off their engine before beginning fueling. "How long are you planning to stay?"

"Who knows? It all depends how long Angus feels it's necessary to have someone around to cover for him."

A twinge of conscience made Rain temporarily put her own worries aside and she murmured, "I saw his cast. What happened?"

"He fell off his roof. Right now, he's counting on me to keep things running smooth until he's better. Lucky for him, I've got all kinds of experience. As an auto mechanic, I mean."

Once again hearing the slyness in his voice, Rain stiffened. "I'll bet you're as handy as pockets on a shirt."

His grin grew feral, exposing teeth impressively white and straight for a man who looked like he lived on whiskey, black coffee and tobacco. "Yes, indeed. Feel free to call on me anytime, being as I'll be staying in that trailer right over there. I've always thought neighbors should take care of each other, don't you?"

It took her a moment to absorb the horror of knowing he would only be a few dozen yards away every day—and night. "On the contrary, I've always had more admiration for the ones who knew how to mind their own business."

"Well, the offer stands. You never know what, er, needs might arise."

No matter what he'd meant, the innuendo was clearer. Incensed, Rain drew herself to her full five feet four inches. "Stay off my property, Mr. Marlowe, and stay away from me."

Too furious to congratulate herself for retaining at least a modicum of dignity, she began to leave. Suddenly, she felt his ironlike grip close around her arm.

Dignity be hanged, she decided.

Three

A blessed surge of adrenaline carried Rain's indignation in its wake. The moment Jake swung her back toward him, pulling her off balance and against his body, she was ready for battle as she'd never been ready before.

"Take your hands off or so help me, I . . . I'll . . ."

"Pay for your gas?"

She stopped pushing against his chest. She blinked up at him. She wanted to die. "Oh, no!" she moaned, aghast. "I forgot."

"So it would seem. Why do you think I stopped you from leaving?"

Was it her imagination or did his voice suddenly take on a gruffer, more whispery quality? It spawned mental flashes of her fantasy lover and sent little shock waves throughout her body. Spooked, she wondered if she could be losing her mind.

No, it was because she'd missed both breakfast and lunch. The small box of raisins she'd found in her desk drawer had helped some, but it couldn't begin to make up for two skipped meals. The heat was a major culprit, too. It surrounded her, was slowly suffocating her. Yes, she assured herself, all rational explanations and none having anything to do with him.

"You're not going to faint on me again, are you?" he asked, sending a new swell of kinetic energy through her.

"Of course not."

"Good, because I have an ironclad rule. One faint per day per distressed damsel. After that there's a surcharge."

The sexy drawl, the way his thumbs stroked in slow, soothing circles, proved the wrong kind of antidote to her temper. Barely stopping herself in time from asking what kind of charge, she curled her hands into fists and willed herself lucid. She would *not* throw her arms around his neck; she would *not* throw caution to the wind.

"I'm fine," she insisted again, although she still sounded anything but convincing. "And technically I didn't faint this morning, either."

Jake's laugh proved an extension of his irreverent behavior. "You have to be the most stubborn, infuriating woman I've ever met."

"Well, if you dislike me so, why don't you leave me alone?" Stronger now, she used that strength to wriggle free.

"Who said anything about disliking you? As a matter of fact, I'm getting somewhat partial to the way your eyes flash whenever you get all hot and bothered."

Tempted to turn the pail of windshield washer fluid over his head, squeegee and all, she reached into her car for her purse. It was thoroughly despicable of him to tease her like this, she fumed, especially since he knew what she'd been through. All but ripping the two bills she owed him from her wallet, she thrust them into his hand and climbed into her car.

"Leaving so soon?"

She prayed for the patience to get away from him without doing or saying something more vile than she already had. She wasn't pleased that the man was single-handedly turning her into a shrew.

Rain groaned to herself when the engine failed to catch. She tried again, only to be humiliated by the sound of grinding gears.

"If you'll turn off your air conditioner, you'll find it puts less strain on your engine."

She knew that. And, if he hadn't been toying with her like a big, lazy cat batting a defenseless mouse between its paws, she would have remembered, too.

Finally the car started. Without a word in parting or a backward glance, she drove off.

"Come again!" he called after her.

Not if she could help it, she vowed with steeping anger. There was a self-service station near the highway, and regardless of the fact that it was three miles out of her way, she planned to trade there until Angus returned and Mr. Jake Marlowe left Stiles for good.

How could Angus be so gullible? She couldn't be the only one to have figured it out; five minutes around the man and anyone had to see he was the worst thing to hit Stiles since the heat wave and drought!

Only belatedly did she realize her fixation moved Gil and Polly into a secondary slot. It proved just another reason to dislike the man.

Jake found it amazing how stubborn the woman could be. For the rest of the day and throughout the night, she not only stayed in her house, she also kept her front door shut. Must have been like an oven in there, he reflected early Sunday afternoon as he watched a young customer approach with a frozen crème pop she'd chosen from the freezer. The turquoise blue color reminded him of his own unpalatable tastes as a boy.

"That looks nice and cool, but are you sure your momma knows you're buying this?" Jake teased gently, taking her money and returning the appropriate change.

"Uh-huh." A solemn nod accompanied the pensive reply.

He couldn't hold back a smile. The little girl was adorable in her yellow dress, even though the smock-style garment had seen countless washings. "Been to church, huh?"

Another nod followed.

He gave her a wink, knowing it was time to let her go before he frightened her. "Well, you take care and enjoy that treat."

Without replying, she raced out the opened door.

Jake watched her trot pony-style to her bike. The ends of her cornrowed hair bobbed up and down, reminding him of the octopus ride he'd once operated at a county fair. As she reached her bike, she maneuvered it in the direction of the path that led through the dry fields to the group of shanty-type houses that unofficially marked the city limits of town. He was learning that a number of the folks from there shopped here because few had second cars to get them into town.

Compassion had him tightening his lips. As unrelenting as the heat was in here, with his own fan on and all the doors open, he knew he had it made compared to his neighbors.

With a sigh, he headed back to the garage. A muffler job was waiting for him, but the heavy air, heat and dust soon convinced him that he wasn't ready to crawl beneath the half ton of steel on wheels. Not yet. He didn't have any problems with claustrophobia, but he couldn't work if sweat kept pouring into his eyes.

He would wait until later this evening to finish it. After the sun set. Since the owner wasn't expecting the truck until tomorrow, it would be all right, time wise.

Instead he wandered outside to the small island by the trailer. Along the way he paused to kick the tire he'd repaired and inflated last night after he'd gotten fed up with rolling off the narrow bed while trying to watch TV.

Satisfied that it seemed to be holding, he continued to the island and rewound the air hose some customer had left on the ground. After looping it properly on its hanger, he picked up the fatter water hose and opened the valve.

Once he let the first few seconds of flow—undoubtedly stinging hot from the sun—offer some relief to the parched ground near the surviving shrubs framing the island, he bent from the waist and let the tepid stream soak his hair. Behind his closed lids he pictured a waterfall in the Washington Cascades. Goose-bump cold. Invigorating.

The relief didn't last long. A quick mouthful of the stuff certainly didn't quench his thirst. He wanted a beer so bad he could taste it. Angus had plenty in a back cooler and Jake knew his new employer wouldn't mind if he indulged; but he had his own sense of what was and what wasn't appropriate while the station was open. He had no intention of putting Angus's faith in him in jeopardy. He settled for cupping his hand and once again rinsing his mouth with the lukewarm water.

Finally, he shut off the tap. Straightening, he raked his hands through his hair. The rivulets of liquid coursing down his neck to his back and chest felt good. But too soon the greedy sun dried it and began baking him again.

Hell, he thought with a chest-deep moan, it's too hot for anything... including sex. Yet the notion had him eyeing Rain's empty driveway. He didn't know why. He didn't want to dwell on it, either.

About to go back inside and turn on the portable black-and-white television set behind the counter, he spotted her car approaching from town. Some wayward mood crept up out of nowhere; the corner of his mouth curled upward.

This morning, when she'd left for church, he'd come out to exchange a few words only to be ignored, more blatantly than when she'd passed him and Angus the other day. He hadn't been surprised; after all, she'd made herself clear as to her feelings, but what did get to him was realizing how much he'd enjoyed teasing her. And looking at her, he had to add, remembering how clean and prim she'd been in her dove gray suit. So maybe he hadn't been wild about all that material in her skirt. There'd been enough yardage there to sew new curtains for half the windows in the trailer. Now, as he watched her park in her driveway and shut off the car's engine, he thought about her preference for figure-hiding, stifling clothes and allowed that they would make anyone uptight and prickly natured.

He much preferred her the way she'd been dressed—*undressed*—yesterday when they'd first met. It was criminal to hide such a delectable body. The moment the car door swung open and she slipped out both legs at once, with a ladylike grace he was fast learning had to be inherent, he was reminded of that. All it took was a glimpse of sleek limbs and his imagination stirred to life. He took the image one step further and pictured her nude, stretched out on cool, pristine sheets only slightly paler than her skin. Yes, she would take a man's breath away.

And she was once again ignoring him.

"Afternoon, Miss Rain!" he shouted, his hands cupped to his mouth. "Been to church?"

She slammed the car door. Hard.

Jake waited for her to get partway up the walk before calling again. "Never thought a fine Christian lady would be mean spirited so soon after services!"

As he'd hoped, that stopped her in her tracks, and to his delight she swung around to face him. "I believe I made myself clear yesterday," she returned formally. "I've nothing to say to you."

That and taxes were blatantly clear, but it did nothing to relieve his boredom. All the church business Angus had told him about had passed a good twenty minutes ago—which also had him wondering what had kept her— and now there were several hours to go before he could close. A man had to find his entertainment any way he could. He'd chosen Miss Rain Neelson.

He scrunched up his face and, holding a hand to his ear, yelled, "Pardon? I didn't quite get that."

"Oh, I think you did."

"No, ma'am." He shook his head with abject earnestness. "Your soft voice isn't strong enough to carry all this way."

He could sense her indecision by the way she hesitated. Thank goodness she was a country girl, he thought fleetingly. She would get eaten alive in a city. But when she began reluctantly retracing her steps to the end of her driveway, he found himself forgetting his concern for her inexperience and fought back a grin.

"Can you hear me now?"

"I think I got the 'you' and 'me' parts. What's the rest? An invitation to lunch?"

One of her baby-fine eyebrows lifted and he knew she'd caught on to him at last. "Swine will ice skate on the town-square pool first, Mr. Marlowe."

Once again she stalked back to the house. He hounded her every step, first with a loud, belly-deep groan of disappointment, then he wheedled and teased. Nothing, however, won another response from her.

As the front door slammed behind her, Jake laughed. But the outburst ended in a sigh. Strange little bird, he mused. Maybe she saw him as rude and unfair with his catcalls, but she couldn't deny he was helping her keep her mind off her worthless ex-fiancé. Then again, he wondered if she even noticed that yet.

He wondered what the hell he was getting into.

The man was worse than an aggravation, Rain concluded in the week that followed, he was a walking insult to decent women. To her at any rate. Granted, since his arrival she hadn't noticed him being as familiar, as *rude* to anyone the way he was with her. But she wished she could forego the honor.

On the following Saturday she was still muttering and almost dropped the special-delivery box marked Fragile that had come in for one of their customers. Carefully lifting it onto the service counter, she took a series of long, deep breaths to collect herself. But even after taking a moment to watch customers amble into the lobby to post letters and bills and check their mailboxes, she thought it debatable as to what was having the greater affect on her deteriorating disposition, Jake Marlowe or the heat.

She despised him for what he was doing. His very presence was turning the town on its ear. Thank goodness the counter was closed today, she thought gloomily. If one more woman walked in and told her how fortunate she was to have such a fascinating man staying across the street from her, she would scream. Bad enough that they'd begun visiting Angus's station under various and sundry pretenses; why did they insist on subjecting her to their giddy chatter as well?

Even the men in town were falling prey, hanging around the garage as though the place was a fountain of information. Jake's wit, his easygoing manner and his jack-of-all-trades talents—as *they* described them—were proving a draw.

Well, not as far as she was concerned.

Rain thought the whole situation disgusting. Most of all she resented him for paying her more attention than everyone else. The last thing she needed or wanted—especially at this inopportune time in her life—was to be set apart from the crowd, made noticeable.

What made it worse was his logic; he only behaved as he did because he knew how unhappy, how uncomfortable it made her. She could tell as much when she looked into his laughing eyes. Somehow he could pick up on her deepest secrets. Most of them anyway. What really terrified her was the thought that he might figure out the newest one, the one that even left her shaking her head.

What would he do if he knew she dreamed of being beautiful, beautiful enough to seriously tempt him?

All by itself, it wasn't an outlandish idea. What was wrong with, just once, knowing how it felt to drive a man crazy with desire? But as simple as it was, it was also bizarre.

No doubt about it, her world had gone topsy-turvy. And, as if her nervous system wasn't already overloaded, she'd heard that Gil and Polly were returning. They'd telephoned Polly's family, advising they would be back Sunday. How would she deal with them on top of everything else?

A muffled call and the sound of pounding on the lobby's glass door drew Rain out of her brooding. She spotted Enid Webster pointing to her granddaddy's pocket watch that she'd pulled from her overall's pocket. Here we go again, she thought, letting herself out from behind the counter and unlocking the door.

"Hate to see you going soft-headed like every other female in this town just because we got a new bull in the pasture," the stocky woman declared.

Rain ignored the insult for the simple reason that she knew it would do her no good, the same way it would do no good to remind Enid that they were closed today. "Morning," she sang in a pleasant, if wistful, voice. "How are you today?"

"Hmph. Maybe that boy Angus hired *is* strapping and handy," the woman continued as though Rain hadn't spoken, thumping her thumb against her chest, "but you remember you heard it first here. He may be stayin' across the street from you, but he ain't the kind to tarry. You mind that, girl."

Rain nodded, repressing the urge to defend herself. It disturbed her enough to think Enid had guessed who she'd been thinking about. Forcing a polite smile on her face, as she'd been doing since the morning after Gil and Polly's elopement, she asked, "Need a stamp?"

The aging tomboy dug rough, callused hands into her pockets again and came out with a rumpled envelope. "This won't get anywhere without one, will it?"

They went through the same routine every Saturday, but today it was too much for Rain. "Why don't you buy a book? You'd save me breaking the rules for you, not to mention yourself the trip down here."

"I don't mind the drive. Gets me away from my troubles," Enid replied, scowling at the stamp Rain drew from her pocket.

Rain licked the back of it and affixed the small square to the envelope for her.

"Prices go up again?"

"No, they're exactly what they were on Wednesday when you bought your last one."

"You guarantee it'll get to where it's going on time?"

"It's a first-class mailing, Enid," Rain explained with hard-won patience. "If *you* mailed it in time, I'm sure it will arrive expeditiously."

The woman snorted. "That ain't saying much. You took eleven days to deliver my grandniece's birthday card to Mobile, Alabama, and I'd sent it off a week early."

Rain heard mutterings of that sort all the time and accepted Enid's ire. Regardless of whether she agreed or disagreed with her, there was nothing she could do about the system outside her branch. She preferred, instead, to change the subject. "How're things on the farm?"

"Won't be any farm if we don't get some rain soon." Enid had inherited her parents' forty acres—not far from Rain's house—and, except for the few months she'd been married back in the sixties, she'd been managing it on her own. "I'm about ready to start raising catfish the way everyone else seems to be doing these days. Looking at water would beat watching your fields turn to straw."

"I heard on the news this morning that there's a thirty percent chance of showers," Rain offered, hoping it would garner one positive remark out of the woman.

"Hmph. Humid as it's getting, they ought to be telling us ninety percent."

Throughout the day numerous people echoed Enid's opinion. And as the day progressed, tempers gained a sharper edge. It only got worse when the clouds began to build up. Most people felt they were nothing short of provoking, a reminder of the precipitation they sorely needed but weren't going to get.

But as agitated as the people filing through the lobby were, it was George who taxed Rain's patience most of all. After refusing to get the mail for a longtime rental-box patron who'd forgotten his key, he snapped at Malva for opening the side door and handing the elderly man the box's contents herself.

"Would you step into my office?" Rain asked him, though her tone left it clear she was ordering him and not requesting.

Disgruntled, he stomped past her. Once she shut the door, he declared, "Just last week you put up the notice warning box renters they were responsible for getting their own mail. Are you going to tell me that now you want me to ignore regulations?"

"Granted, it's our responsibility to see that regulations are carried out properly—" Rain took her place behind her desk to help her mentally retain her authority "—but I feel that if you have a special case like Mr. Herman, who's well past eighty and has been a resident of this town for longer than you've been on this planet, it's not going to hurt anyone to make a minor exception. Provided," she added when George opened his mouth to speak, "it's not creating an inconvenience to any other customer."

"Sure. Start there and watch what follows."

"The subject's closed," Rain said quietly, only to raise her hand. "On second thought, there is something else. I don't want to hear you speaking to Malva with such disrespect again."

"You two're getting to be regular chums, aren't you?" George said, all but sneering.

Rain cocked an eyebrow and folded her arms beneath her breasts. "I beg your pardon?"

"I think I was clear enough. Things have been going on in this office that make it apparent my job as supervisor is in jeopardy. But I want you to know that if you try to promote her over me, I'm going to file a complaint."

The ludicrousness of his accusation left Rain wanting to laugh, except that she knew the repercussions would be anything but funny. "George..." She sighed. "Take the rest of the afternoon off and go home. Obviously, the heat's taking its toll on your ability to rationalize. Whatever gave you the idea that I intend to promote anyone over you?"

"You're not?"

"No, I'm not. Contrary to what you may think, when you're not out to make someone else look bad, I feel you're an excellent worker. Now I've known since day one that you're resentful of having to take orders from a woman—"

"So now you're accusing me of being prejudiced?"

Rain clenched her teeth together and silently counted to twenty. "I'm stating the facts as I see them. George, we're a small branch. We can't afford such volatile personality conflicts as those you're instigating. We rely on each other too much. Please, do as I suggested, take the rest of the afternoon off and see if you can't let some of your bitterness go. Why not drive up to Oxford and take your wife for a nice, relaxing evening out?''

His whole bearing grew stiff. ''I have no choice but to listen to you around here, but kindly keep your nose out of my personal life. Especially since you're hardly in a position to give advice about relationships.''

But he did leave. Rain sighed with relief, certain that had he stayed she would have done something foolish—like cry. How cruel, she thought, watching him snatch up his black lunch pail and charge out the back door, ignoring Bud's comic complaints about being abandoned. What right did one person have to hurt another so recklessly?

If his intent had been to remind her of her inadequacies, however, he'd succeeded several times over. But even his display of cruelty could be topped; Rain found that out when Malva brought her the postcard minutes before they locked up for the evening.

''I thought I'd wait as long as I could before I ruined your day.''

Rain tried not to focus on the picture of flamingos and the famous logo of the Florida theme park in the photo. Instead she gave the other woman a dry smile. ''What do you want to bet it doesn't say, 'Wish you were here'?''

''I took it from George before he could read the whole thing,'' Malva told her. ''I think that's the real reason he got mad.'' Before Rain could do more than murmur her thanks, Malva was heading out the door. Then, as though changing her mind, she turned back. ''If I was you,'' she added more cautiously, ''I wouldn't read it. I'd rip it up and throw it away. Ain't no reason to let those people bother you no more.''

She had a point. But whether she was a glutton for punishment or simply curious, Rain decided she had to find out what creative communication Polly and Gil had sent her.

The moment she flipped over the postcard she recognized the large, round, childlike handwriting as Polly's—even before she glanced down at the signature signed with the tag, "Love." She drew a deep breath in preparation and read the rest.

Rain, By now you know I've become Mrs. Gilbert Wakefield. Please don't hate me because he loved me more than he did you. You're so strong and self-reliant, you're not afraid to be alone as I am.

Having a fantastic time. Gil is spoiling me rotten and I don't want to leave. But I promise we'll see you soon. I really would like us to talk and clear the air.

"No need to hurry on my account," she muttered, tossing the postcard on top of the rest of her mail.

She had spilled her last tears over those two. Once she got to the house, she would do as Malva suggested and rip the thing into tiny pieces, ceremoniously turning them into the ashes they deserved to be.

Nonetheless, every muscle in her body ached from tension by the time she drove home, every nerve was stretched to its limit. As a result, when she rounded the turn to where she could see Angus's garage, it relieved her to discover her other "headache" was busy with a customer and probably wouldn't be able to bother her.

Perfect, she thought, today would not be a good day for him to test the limits of her patience. But once she identified the red convertible and the shimmering waves of silver-blond hair as Lena Raymond, she knew there was no threat of that happening.

White short-shorts stretched to their maximum while Lena bent low to inspect whatever Jake was pointing out at the back of her car. More than likely, Rain thought with a waspishness that she refused to feel guilty over, Lena was whispering directions to finding her spare house key.

On the other hand, why shouldn't she? The woman may have been the second wife of the town's late mayor, but she was hardly of an age to be relegated to a rocking chair at the county rest home. In fact, everyone knew it was Lena's particular talent to sniff out a new eligible man in Stiles. Rain thought the woman had a keener nose than Norm's blue-tick hound. That would also explain why Lena had driven all the way across town when everyone knew she had her cleaning lady's muscle-bound son to handle technicalities such as seeing that she had plenty of superunleaded in her tank.

Fine. She and Jake deserved each other, Rain thought, her mood growing more acerbic. She parked, and then made tracks for the front door. But try as she might, she couldn't keep from glancing across the street one more time, only to fight back a sound of disdain. She hoped Lena got a heat rash from those shorts chafing her tender parts.

Once inside, she threw her things on the coffee table and proceeded to open every door and window in order to expel the pent-up heat. After that she hurried to her bedroom and stripped off her damp work clothes, tugged on a short-sleeved blouse and a pair of cotton slacks. But her thoughts remained as volatile as her movements.

Admit it, she finally scolded herself, *you wish you had the nerve to show everyone how wrong they are about you.* Polly and Gil...they'd assumed too much. And, oh, to call Jake Marlowe's bluff and prove she wasn't a scaredy-cat or a dull little mouse or any of the things he and everyone else around here alluded about her through tone or behavior. They were lucky she didn't show them all the passionate and aggressive woman she really was.

How? an inner voice challenged. She turned to face her mirror. *Look at yourself. Who'd want you?*

Rain's fight drained out of her. It was true; she looked like...like a frump. An uptight, matronly bore. Why else did she dress in slacks and a button-up blouse in this heat? Why wear a bra in the privacy of her own home?

Turning away from the mirror, she stripped off the offending items and tossed them over a chair. Then she pensively considered the contents of her closet. What she saw there depressed her.

Maybe she'd been ignoring this aspect of her life for too long. She needn't get carried away and change her work wardrobe—it was important to look professional—but what kept her from dressing for herself at home?

She snatched out the short silky sleeper she'd planned to wear to bed tonight. Cut in a tank-top style, the seafoam-on-sapphire top was loose and long enough to get away with just wearing her panties beneath it. Most important, however, it felt deliciously cool against her skin.

"Much better," she murmured, heading for the kitchen. Now she needed a tall ice-packed glass of tea, or maybe she would make that multiflavored juice concentrate she'd purchased on impulse a few weeks ago and had yet to open.

Too hot to think about food, she finally settled down on her couch to read one of the new tempestuous paperbacks she'd also purchased on impulse during that shopping trip. She soon discovered it was a pleasant break to focus on someone else's problems for a change. Who knows, she mused, maybe the characters would give her a hint as to what to do with her own life.

Two chapters into the story, thoroughly engrossed with the strength and passion of the heroine, she heard the first rumble of thunder.

It couldn't be, Jake thought. They weren't that lucky to get any relief from this steam bath. Nevertheless, he went to the front of the trailer and bent over the kitchen table to look out the louvered windows. Sure enough, the sky to the west had turned to an angry slate blue.

As a bolt of lightning shot down from the clouds, he whistled softly and headed for the TV. It looked threatening enough for more than rain and he wanted to see if the local station had them under some kind of weather warning.

He'd closed the garage only minutes ago and had planned to shove a frozen dinner in the microwave. Not that he felt like eating, he thought, taking another swallow of his beer.

A special-report logo came over the screen, followed by the familiar face of the station's meteorologist. He announced a severe storm warning had been issued for the Oxford area, including their county.

As heavy droplets began falling, sounding like lead bearings on the trailer's roof, Jake returned to the windows. No, he decided, there was no way they were going to miss this one. That was fine with him, but when seconds later the skies opened to a downpour and a gust of wind hit the side of the trailer with the strength to rock it, he extended his opinion to worry about a tornado. If one came, a trailer would be the last place he wanted to be.

But where to go? He opened the door and eyed the garage. Tin flapped like wash on a clothesline and even the plywood doors seemed to be testing the nails that held them in place.

Uh-uh, he thought and glanced across to Rain's house.

Hail began to fall. Although only pea size, it would probably hurt like hell. On the other hand, her house was looking more and more inviting with every minute. It definitely was the place to be if he wanted to ensure his safety against high winds.

He went back to the refrigerator and snatched up the rest of his six-pack. Next he shut off everything electrical. Finally he jumped down onto the still-warm cement, slammed the door behind himself and ran.

Four

His dash across the street took no more than twenty seconds, but by the time Jake reached Rain's driveway his hair and clothes were plastered to him. By the time he yanked at the screen door and rushed into her house, he was drenched.

An atmosphere of dusk and shadows enveloped him, making it difficult to see. If not for the few candles on the corner table by the couch where Rain sat, it might have taken him longer to spot her. Sat, hell, he amended, feeling the breath sucked out of him at the same instant she uttered a strangled yelp and bolted upright. Where she lay.

"What do you think you're doing?"

Good thing she had no ambitions for a stage career, he mused. Her words were meant to reflect indignation, but the panic in her voice and shocked expression on her face more closely reflected a woman scared half out of her wits and expecting the worst. However, when he opened his mouth to inform her that deflowering the local post-mistress wasn't high on his list of priorities at the moment, the words wouldn't come out. He'd suffered some kind of a short circuit and it was all her fault.

The other Rain was back. Gone were the yards of clothing, the pins restricting her hair, the sensible shoes. This Rain wore a brushstroke of bluish green that spawned whimsical thoughts of mermaids and dragon-fly wings. Its low cut exposed an elegant length of neck, and its short length exhibited legs that made him think of less proper, less tame things. Like a man rising from a coma, he simply stood there and stared.

"I don't believe your nerve," she continued, shifting the book she'd been reading to her chest. As coverings went, it made an inadequate choice, doing little to hide her braless state; and when a gust of cooler air flowed through the door and windows—or dare he believe his presence affected her so?—it made her nipples tighten provocatively.

"And I don't believe *you*," he shot back. "Haven't you been paying attention to what's going on outside?" He glanced at the cocktail glass on the coffee table, briefly wondering if the woman was a closet lush, then quickly rejected the idea. He'd wager his bike that the juicelike contents were strictly that and nothing more.

"Of course, I have. We're finally getting a shower."

"We're under a severe weather warning." He stepped over to the low table and set down his beer beside what looked to be her mail. "That must be some book if it's blocked out how all hell's breaking loose out there. Want to take turns reading the good parts to each other, or aren't there any?"

"Get out."

Instead, Jake raked his hands through his hair, combing out rainwater and sending a new stream down his back. "Under normal circumstances I'd oblige you, but I'm more afraid of a tornado than I am of whatever you're likely to do."

"Then let me try to change your mind. You have exactly ten seconds to take your beer and get out of here or I'm going to call the—" The sudden wail of the town's recently installed tornado warning siren cut her off. "Oh, my word!" She leapt from the couch and joined him at the door. "We really are under a warning."

"That's what I've been trying to tell you." But Jake didn't bother viewing the deteriorating weather as she did. He'd lost interest in the intensifying downpour, the flashes of sheet lightning and forked bolts brightening the sky. He found it more interesting to study the way her hair fell in soft waves, how it brushed against her delicate collarbone. Her slightest movement brought a phantom trace of lily of the valley drifting up to tease his senses, and each strand of silky, shining hair tempted him to reach out and touch. "You still want me to go back to that tin coffin over there?" he asked, lowering his inspection to watch the wind press her wispy gown across pert, taut breasts.

"I had no idea it had gotten this bad."

Feeling his body stirring, Jake thought about how bad it could get. A gust of wind carried rain through the screen, and he took instant advantage. Taking hold of her arms, he urged her back from the door. "You shouldn't stand so close," he said, schooling his voice to hide his lascivious fantasies. The weather, seemingly on his side, sent a bolt of lightning spearing from the sky and aiming for somewhere nearby.

Rain cringed against him, but before Jake could take advantage, she caught herself and moved farther into the room. "Um, they say you should go to the most secure part of the house."

"What?"

"The hallway?" she shouted to be heard over the warning siren and a deafening peal of thunder.

The hallway held promise. Jake could visualize himself backing her against a wall and kissing her until, weak-kneed, she would cling to him. But once given its lead, his imagination turned relentless. "They say a closet is better."

"I do keep that one ready." She indicated the door opposite her bedroom. "But it's not set up to hold more than one person."

The wind and rain seemed determined to work in his favor. Combined, they created a roar that made her faint protest meaningless. When the cacophony was intensified by the sound of something banging against the house, Rain simply grabbed Jake's arm. "We'll make due," she told him, leading him to the closet.

With boxes stacked on either side of the walls and coats in between, Jake quickly determined she'd been right: they were going to be cramped. He loved it. "Perfect!" he declared, then toned down his enthusiasm with, "We'll be much safer here."

How safe was a rhetorical question. Not very, he suspected, if one cared about minor details such as breathing, or if one had an aversion to being baked like a soufflé. Nevertheless, he pushed the coats aside and angled his long length into the cubbyhole in the middle. But once Rain followed, shutting the door behind herself, his discomfort mellowed considerably. Mercy, he groaned silently, could she mollify him.

In thick-aired darkness they twisted and squirmed. Body parts became intimately acquainted with body parts. Mere breathing required the strategy of an athletic sport.

"I think if I turn this way..." Rain suggested, her tone anything but confident.

Jake tried not to groan at the intimacy her position created. "Ah . . . you might want to get your hand away from my . . ."

"Sorry. Why don't I move my leg over here . . . ?"

After her third attempt to avoid straddling his thigh, he took hold of her waist and held her still. "Honey, if you don't stop doing that, you're going to have me embarrassing myself."

He heard her breath catch and knew she understood. "This isn't going to work," she announced with a postmistress's authority.

"Sure it will. Stop trying to complicate things and stand still."

"But you're soaking wet and making me wet, too!"

Jake grinned in the darkness. "Miss Rain, how you do talk."

"That does it. I'm out of here."

"Wait!" He tightened his hold of her. "Listen . . . man, it's sounding bad out there now."

That much was true. The wind roared, and the way thunder shook the house it seemed the worst of the storm was right over them. He could almost feel Rain's resignation.

"All right," she muttered, "but would you mind removing your hands?"

"Yes, I think I would since it's the only way I can keep you from permanently crippling me. By the way, has anyone ever told you that you have a true Southern belle's waist?'' When she failed to respond, instead fumbling for something on the boxes behind him, he sighed good-naturedly. "Now what are you looking for?"

"A flashlight. I thought there was one in this tote and . . . here it is."

She lit it and the beam caught him straight in the eyes. Grimacing, he pushed the flashlight away. "Is that thing necessary?"

"Yes, because you behave marginally better when I can see you. And if you don't, I plan to beat you with this."

"It's a tough choice, but I think I liked you better when you were acquainting yourself with my, er, belt buckle."

For a moment scathing silence reigned. Finally she ground out, "Do you ever think about anything besides sex?"

"Not when you're around."

She didn't reply, but Jake knew the exact moment she reached for the doorknob. He closed a hand around her wrist and tugged, trapping it between their bodies. The wrestling match resumed and in the skirmish that followed she dropped the light.

Once again they were cast in darkness.

"Let me go this instant," she demanded.

"Stop rubbing against me as though we're on a ten-minute date and I will."

He could feel her breath hot and hard against his chest, her anger and frustration in every tight muscle of her body. Finally, with a barely audible whimper, she slumped against him pressing her forehead against his shoulder. "I truly despise you," she said through clenched teeth.

Tempted to press his lips to her fragrant hair, Jake leaned his head back into the coats and closed his eyes.

"No you don't. That's our problem. We're attracted to each other, but you're afraid to do anything about it."

"Good grief." Brief laughter filled the stifling cubicle. "You certainly are full of yourself."

Damn, but she would be hell to play chess with. Here he had her in a classic "check" position, and she still refused to surrender. Torn between frustration and admiration, he replied, "Are you suggesting you haven't thought about what it would be like if we made love? Ah-ah-ah," he added, aware of the rising heat and stiffness in her body, "before you start denying it, remember that I'm the guy who taught you to French kiss."

"You have the manners of an alley cat."

"What can I tell you, it's a genetic condition."

"Don't drag your family into this."

"Facts are facts. Remember my fiancée and my brother? What I didn't get around to telling you was that he didn't fight her off with a stick. Even our folks had one-track minds. They married two weeks after their first date. But most interesting was my grandparents. Now there's a tale that would strike a match under your hormones."

"Spare me."

Little puritan, Jake thought grinning again. "Have it your way, but the point is I'm blameless."

"You're disturbed."

"That's partly *your* fault." He gave up trying to resist the temptation to touch her hair. It was softer against his cheek than he'd imagined, and carried the same fragrance that had been haunting him. "It comes from wanting your mouth under mine again," he murmured gruffly. "Care to put me out of my misery?"

"I'd rather take my chances with a tornado."

He didn't have to see to know she'd flung her head back, or that their lips were close. He could feel them, their heat mere centimeters away. Awareness created its own electricity, one he wanted to relish thoroughly before satisfying the hunger she kept stirring within him. "Okay, fight it," he continued, shifting the leg thrust between hers ever so slightly. His knee stroked her inner thigh. "It'll only make the end result all the more exciting."

"In your dreams maybe."

A crash in the living room ended his opportunity for a comeback. They both leaned toward the door and listened. Could there be a tornado after all? Jake wondered.

"I'm going to check," Rain announced.

"Don't be ridiculous."

"I forgot to blow out the candles. What if they tipped over and started a fire?" Pushing against his chest, she grappled for the doorknob and this time succeeded in thrusting it open. As slippery as a spring trout, she scrambled over him and into the living room.

Following with far less enthusiasm, the first thing he spotted was the floor lamp. The flapping drapes had knocked it over, resulting in a domino effect; but the damage appeared to be minimal. As Rain went to blow out the candles, he stooped to pick up the scattered envelopes and magazines that had fallen off the coffee table.

The last item turned out to be a postcard. He didn't mean to read the back; his gaze simply zeroed in on the name 'Gil' and the rest just happened.

No wonder she'd been moody and ready for combat, he thought shaking his head over the thinly disguised taunting from her so-called friend. This kind of twisting-the-knife-in-the-back would sour anyone's disposition.

"Give me that!"

Rain snatched it out of his hands. He knew better than to offer an excuse for his nosiness, but felt a need to say something. "I'm sorry. I mean about the way they hurt you."

"I don't want your pity." She began ripping the crumpled card into shreds. "I'm sick... and ... tired of people always looking at me as though I'm some object of misfortune."

"That wasn't the way I was looking at you."

"No, of course not." Her eyes blazed and the room hummed with her overflowing fury. "And what was all that ridiculousness in the closet about? Passion?"

A long, vibrating peal of thunder shook the house, a perfect underscoring of her deep-seated anger. But Jake was nearing the end of his patience as well. "Exactly. The one thing you better know about me is that I don't do charity work, honey."

"Right. Because I'm so irresistible."

"When you don't have a chip on your shoulder, yeah."

Rain couldn't believe she could say such horrible things; but now that they were coming out of her, she didn't seem able to stop, either. It was as though twenty-nine years of repressed emotions were bubbling to the surface. "Look who's talking, Mr. Self-Possessed himself. At least I'm not out to prove something with every live wire I pass."

"What's that supposed to mean?"

She knew she should respect the dangerous low note that suddenly entered his voice. She should be concerned with the way his facial muscles froze as though they'd turned to granite, and the way his gray eyes were turning as dark as the room. But there was no reversing the adrenaline surging through her and she dismissed all those warning signals.

"You're still trying to prove the woman who chose your brother over you made a mistake," she charged recklessly. "You drift from town to town turning every head you can, making hearts race with your devilish smile and your intense stares, until you run out of challenges and decide to move on. Isn't that the way it goes?"

"You seem to have all the answers."

"And the sense to recognize a philanderer when I see one." She touched her index finger to her chest. "Well, you're not going to make me into another notch on your belt, Mr. Marlowe, because regardless of how I may appear to you, I am not desperate to take a man to bed. Certainly not the first no-account drifter who rambles into town. Yes, Gilbert Wakefield dumped me for my best friend, but that has nothing, *nothing* to do with who I am, and it's *his* loss not to have figured that out."

Jake matched her glare for glare. "So you can talk tough. But way down deep I'll bet you haven't a clue as to what you really want or how to get it if you did."

Incensed, Rain stepped toward him and flung her head back to meet his challenge. "Mister, if I decided you were *it*, I'd be the one experience you'd never forget."

"Prove it."

The soft-spoken words were a shot across a ship's bow, a line drawn in the sand. Rain's heart, which hadn't come down out of her throat since he'd stormed into her house, now threatened to leap from her body altogether. *Oh*, she fumed, *he was being utterly outrageous*.

But he was also tempting her... damn him for tempting her.

She wanted him. She'd tried not to. She remained convinced she hated him as much as she'd claimed before, but those hormones he'd talked about didn't need heating; in that respect she appeared to be no different than the rest of her sex. She yearned to know what it would be like to cast caution to the wind and abandon herself to the emotions he incited so effortlessly.

But how could she? She'd been raised to be a good girl. Her beautiful but strict mother had instilled the strongest possible moral code in her, which meant, besides shocking herself by even considering having an affair, that a drifter was the last person she should be saying these things to, especially in this day and age.

On the other hand, he would be perfect. He would leave soon, sparing her the ordeal of having to forever face her one moment of impulsiveness. And he was perfect in another way, too, because he was the first, the only man who'd ever made her feel so feminine, so desirable, so alive. Not even Gil had managed to do that.

Rain could tell by the way he narrowed his eyes that he sensed the turn in her thoughts. It wasn't a comforting look, until she noted how tense her silent stare made him. His chest rose and fell with his every breath as though he couldn't get enough air. His nostrils flared like a predator locking in on the scent of change. There, too, he was right: there was change—her decision hovered between them.

"Come here, Rain."

She ignored his soft-spoken command. Thunder rolled, the heavens continued to deliver what the earth had been yearning for and she lifted her chin higher, determined to wait for everything—or else take nothing.

"I have to know you want this," he explained gruffly.

"And I need to trust you won't treat me like a . . ." So abhorrent was the thought, she couldn't even bring herself to say the word.

"I've never treated a woman with disrespect. I'm not about to start with my first virgin. Come here, Rain," he said again, this time more gently.

No, she thought, she wouldn't be undone by tenderness either. When she stepped toward him, she took hold of a fistful of his T-shirt, so determined was she to make him understand. "I mean to use you. It's only fair to make it reciprocal. Joint need, joint desire." It wasn't the worst reason in the world for two strangers to come together, was it? "Agreed?" she asked, almost getting the word out without her voice quaking. Almost, but not quite.

She waited and parted her lips to suck in the sweet air flooding the room, threatening to drug her. Then she changed her mind and held her breath. She wouldn't be seduced. This would be a conscious, free decision, she insisted to herself as she waited for his reply.

Or lightning to strike her dead.

Or a tornado to sweep them both to perdition.

But the lightning stayed outside and no tornado formed, although the storm lingered, raged. Yet none of it could compare with their own battle of wills.

"Agreed?" she asked again.

Still Jake refused to answer.

Finally, ready to retreat from her foolishness, Rain released his shirt. Only then did his head descend. Only then did he claim her mouth with his.

Like a prisoner exploring freedom for the first time, she went up on tiptoe and wrapped her arms around his neck. The force and intimacy of her body connecting with his won her a groan from him and soon, blissfully soon, came his arms closing around her, crushing her to him. That erased all remaining doubts.

His grip was like a vise, but she didn't mind. Her own was no less demanding. When he nipped at her lip, she bit back. When he thrust his tongue deep into her mouth, she drew him deeper while arching her hips into the powerful thrust of his. What she didn't expect was his reaction. Her bold honesty drove him wild and she almost lost confidence when the hands that had been moving restlessly up and down her back, slid low and cupped her hips, lifting her until she was cradling his fierce arousal.

He was the one to break the kiss, the one to stare into her eyes as though seeing someone new, a stranger for the first time. "Who are you?" he ground out, at once wary, yet intrigued.

She saw it all and it thrilled her. This was what she'd been wanting. "Don't talk," she replied, using one finger to trace the line that ran parallel to his mouth. "Just show me what it's like to burn."

Something flickered in his eyes. Surprise? Respect? She didn't have time to analyze; as quickly as it came, his eyes grew dark again and he bent to press his lips against her neck.

"Talking's part of what makes it good, Rain. A man tells a woman she smells like flowers and tastes like sin."

"Because he thinks she needs to hear that?"

"Because he wants to get inside her more than he wants his next breath."

"Do I smell like flowers and taste like sin?" she asked, filing his wicked, thrilling words away in her deepest, most personal memory banks.

"Lady-girl, you're like nothing there's ever been. I have a feeling you're going to go straight to my head."

Yes, she thought, enjoying his gruff whisper. She wanted that so much the mere thought made her throat drier than she thought possible. "And how do you taste?" she whispered back.

"Oh, honey, I *am* sin. Taste me."

For a moment she felt lost. Where did one begin? She'd spoken bravely, but she didn't know the first thing about seducing a man. What's more, he remained so...dressed.

As though he understood, he momentarily released her and stripped off his T-shirt. "Better?" he murmured, drawing her back against him.

"Much." Rain gazed in silence and wonder. He was beautiful. Bronzed and lean, yet muscular. The dusky hairs across his chest weren't dense, but they drew her attention the most and she nuzzled them before placing an openmouthed kiss against his heart.

Sweat and man combined to tease her taste buds. His thudding heart gave her confidence. "Is that the right way?" she murmured, gazing up at him from beneath her eyelashes.

"The best news of all," he replied, brushing her hair back from her temples, "is that there isn't any right or wrong way. You do whatever gives you pleasure."

And he showed her another side of that pleasure by imprisoning her head with his hands and kissing her again. This time he licked and suckled her lips before delving deeper. By then Rain was ready for more, her craving relayed by her fingers restlessly exploring his shoulders and chest, then sliding up to grip the hair at his nape. Her low moan verbalized her eagerness.

As though he'd been waiting for precisely this response, he tightened his arms more possessively around her until her breasts were crushed against his chest and her tongue tangled with his. Then he repeated the mind-drugging kiss he'd given her that first day.

He would have seduced her there and then had she not already made up her mind that he was the one to teach her what she wanted to know. The taste of him was heady. The sensations he brought her with his hands and mouth made her forget she was skinny and small and plain. By the time he moved on to explore the smoothness of her cheek and the length of her throat, she could barely stand.

"Feeling a bit light-headed?"

With his head bowed to trace the line of her collarbone, she almost missed hearing the smile in his voice. Rather than feeling annoyed, she found it reassuring; she did, after all, want him to enjoy himself, too.

"A little."

"Want to lie down?"

She thought about the carpet and some of her ardor cooled. In the next instant she felt herself lifted high in his arms, the same way he'd carried her on the day they'd met.

Jake laughed softly as he carried her into the bedroom.

"What's so funny?"

"You, the expression on your face. Think I'm so crass I'd let your first time be on the floor?"

He set her on the bed so that she balanced on her knees and, grasping her shoulders, smiled down at her. Touched by his thoughtfulness, Rain smiled back. "I was more concerned about the open door," she confessed. "I should go and lock it just in case."

"Forget the door, we need the air. Besides," he added, stroking his hands along the straps of her gown, "you're supposed to be concentrating on me."

"I was. I..." Her breath caught again when his hands moved downward and he brushed the backs of his fingers over her breasts. "I am," she continued more unsteadily.

"Sensitive," he murmured, his look approving. "Do you know when I first saw you in this I had the fleeting impression I was in the wrong house?"

"It felt too hot for clothes."

"It still is."

Her throat closed up on her, her courage slipped. No one had ever seen her nude except her doctor in Oxford, who was a woman. Even then it had always been in discreet sections, a shift of the sheet here, a lift there. That was hardly going to be the case with Jake.

"No need to be frightened," he told her, taking hold of her hands. He brought each to his mouth for an intense, hot kiss before drawing them across his chest, down his flat, hard belly to his belt buckle. "I don't mind going first."

His gaze held hers and she supposed it was the warmth in his eyes that gave her her courage back. "No." She slid her hands from beneath his, her nails scraping over his fullness. "We'll do it together."

He didn't reply. He didn't have to. When he began undoing the buckle, she decided that as usual, action spoke louder than words.

She swallowed, took firm hold of the hem of her gown and lifted. For a moment she was blinded, but after she flung the filmy covering to the end of the bed and shook her hair out of her eyes, she found Jake in the process of sitting down beside her. He dropped his jeans and shifted around to face her.

A shiver of excitement and desire raced through her. He was now incredibly, magnificently naked, and she was almost nude herself. What's more, his turning brought his mouth within inches of her right breast. Grateful for the expression of intense desire on his face, it seemed the most inevitable and necessary thing in the world to lean forward and offer herself to him.

He didn't disappoint. With a muffled sound, he covered her with his mouth.

An overwhelming wave of pleasure swept over her. Never had she known, dreamed, anything could take her so far so quickly. She had to grip his shoulders to keep from crumbling against him. It was divine, she thought, letting her eyelids drift shut, her head drop back. All the while, arrows of painfully exquisite sensation shot through her body.

"Sweet heaven," Jake muttered, nuzzling her before tasting her again. "It's criminal to think how you hide yourself behind all those clothes."

"You don't understand. I'm . . . too small," she managed.

He cupped her in his hand. "Bull. You're perfect. And you feel . . ."

He didn't finish because he again became absorbed in her shape and textures. Rain didn't mind. What he was doing to her, bringing her, proved far more flattering and reassuring than any words. So much so that when he shifted to perform the same ministrations on her other breast, she whispered, "Yes . . . oh, yes."

Wind whipped into the room, adding its own caresses to her fever-dampened body. Feeling more confident and erotic with every passing moment, Rain clasped the back of Jake's head and arched backward.

She had no idea what she was inviting until she felt his hands slide down to grip her hips, and his mouth follow, coursing a hot trail along the bowed line of her body.

When she felt his teeth on the elastic border of her plain cotton panties, she barely stifled a strangled moan and collapsed onto the bed.

Jake followed, aligning his body to hers. "Too much?" he asked, his look so hungry she wondered whether he would stop if she admitted it was.

"I . . . It's powerful, that's all."

"And it cost you your concentration a bit," he added, using hands and mouth to begin a new journey over her tingling skin. "Were you remembering what it was like with *him?*"

"No."

His hand might as well have been a flame the way it scorched a path up the inside of her thigh to cup her intimately. Rain could barely think, let alone breathe. "Did he ever touch you like this?" he continued, relentless.

Rain couldn't keep still. Her body rose of its own choice to ask and offer. "I don't want to . . . talk about him," she moaned, instinctively flexing muscles to keep him close.

Jake muttered something unintelligible and rolled onto his back growling, "On second thought, neither do I. Come here," he coaxed, taking her with him. "I need to feel you against me."

She'd never been on top of a man before like this and the stark intimacy was shocking, but at the same time exhilarating. If she had any doubts, any hesitation, the expression of unmitigated desire on his face vanquished them.

When she writhed, trying to get closer yet, Jake swore, then pleaded, "Don't stop." He slid his hands below elastic, clasped her bottom and taught her how a slower rhythm could enhance the incredible feelings. "Don't stop. Yeah . . . damn, that's wonderful."

Wonderful, but still not enough. Rain felt both of their bodies liquefying and wondered how long either of them could keep up this torment. "I want you," she said, moaning against the ache that gripped her womb. "Please, Jake?"

"I'm too close," he replied grimly. "Let me take care of you first."

She didn't understand, but he quickly showed her. Rolling her back onto the bed, he stripped her of that last vestige of modesty. Then he slipped two fingers into the damp curls he'd exposed.

"Relax for me, Lady Rain. It'll make it better." He hovered over her, searching her face. His smile was tight, yet encouraging; his eyes were flinty yet filled with admiration. "Jeez, you're burning up. So hot and so very tight."

"Jake...this isn't what I...*oh*."

"Ride it out, honey. Give yourself this and we'll worry about me after."

After? She didn't think she was going to survive *this*, but she had to trust him because her body was already defying her. Clutching his upper arms, she let him race her to the first summit. Then she was beyond it, knowing nothing but the explosions of pleasure rocking her body.

She lost all track of time. Eventually, however, she determined the rushing sound in her ears wasn't her blood as she'd supposed, but the rain continuing to come down steadily. Next she grew aware of how Jake held her, folded against him with a protectiveness and caring she would never have believed him capable of.

As if he felt her gaze, he glanced down at her. "Well?" he murmured, a crooked smile curving his lips. "Curiosity quenched?"

He may have fooled her before, but not this time. She could see the tension shadowing his eyes as easily as she felt his hot, aroused body branding her hip. As touched as she was to realize he would let things stop here, she understood what it cost him, just as she understood that so far, he'd been doing the seducing, not her.

"Not quite," she replied softly, reaching down to take him in her hand. The shudder that raced through his body was a gift in itself; the relief and gratitude softening his eyes proved a reward that threatened to melt her heart. "I think there's supposed to be an epilogue to this story, don't you?"

Rather than reply, he shifted to reach for his jeans. Even with her lack of experience, Rain understood what he was getting and found his conscientiousness for her safety touching. Soon afterward he rose over her.

"It's been a while for me and I've got an appetite that may scare you," he warned, his voice raw and husky.

She met his intent gaze with as much honesty as she could. "I'm not afraid."

"Okay." With his slightest move a muscle twitched in his cheek. As a fine sheen of sweat broke out on his brow and upper lip, he drew a long breath. "Okay. You want to scream, you scream." Cautiously, he settled between her legs. "You want to bite, you can do that, too," he continued more hoarsely, as he slowly made a place for himself inside her.

Rain struggled with the urge to close her eyes against the unbelievable sensation of being filled and filled until even the breath seemed to be squeezed from her lungs. "All I want is to feel you," she said, reaching to draw him closer.

It never hurt. Not much at any rate. His guttural comments—oaths, curses—proved more shocking, as were the emotions she watched flicker across his face. Then he began the deeper thrusts she quickly realized he'd been denying himself. It reignited her desire faster than she'd believed possible.

Sensing a new plateau, she began to move beneath him, undulating to an age-old dance that was born of pure instinct. Eager to soar beyond, she answered some of his murmurings with her own entreaties.

"More woman than a man could have imagined," Jake muttered, bending to press his mouth to her breast.

She wanted it to last forever, but as he warned again, he was too close. And she didn't help. She wrapped her legs around his waist and begged him for everything....

By the time he rolled away from her and she stopped trembling, the storm had passed and an anticlimactic silence hovered in the air.

"Rain?" he asked, just when she thought she couldn't bear the quiet any longer.

"Yes?"

"Was this what you wanted?"

"Yes."

"All that you wanted?"

She didn't know how to answer him.

"Okay, let me put it this way," he said, rising on an elbow and gazing down at her. "What if I want you again?"

Five

"*What do you mean?*"

Like a ghost, Rain's words haunted Jake well into the
night. By the time the fluorescent digits on Angus's bed-
side clock read 2:17 in the morning he was still tossing
and turning on the trailer's uncomfortably narrow cot.
All he could do was remember the warmth and sensual
comfort of being with her. All he could think of was how
fantastic it had been to initiate her into womanhood, only
to lose himself in her passionate response to him.

He'd been startled to realize he hadn't been ready to
leave, at least not so soon. But she hadn't given him a
choice. She'd exhibited strength where he'd shown a
definite lack of restraint and common sense. He should
be grateful to her for her levelheadedness. So why, instead, was he feeling rotten and rejected?

Again and again he replayed the scene that had pre-
ceded his return to his "bachelor quarters." No matter

how many times he went over it, the end result came out the same: he'd been a fool to let himself get too caught up in her, and he had no business feeling as though she was treating him like a one-night stand. But he had and he did.

With an incredulous laugh, Jake rolled onto his back and stared up at the ceiling, illuminated by the garage's security lights, to a dreary expanse of mottled gray. Strangely enough, it suited the weather and his mood perfectly.

Beyond the rain-soaked screens and opened louvered windows, the night was a mind-numbing, bumper sticker-wrinkling mess. While not exactly hot, the surprise downpour hadn't cooled things off much, either. What it had done was tease.

The way Rain's investigation into her sexuality had been a tease.

The way thinking about her was a tease.

He groaned. He wanted. He fought the wanting.

Fine, he told himself, grasping at some point of logic. So it had happened. Maybe it was even necessary. Terrific. But it was over.

"What if I want you again?"

He pressed his palms against his tightly shut eyes. If only he could stop hearing that damned question, stop seeing the way they'd been together, seeing her blossom under the encouragement of his hands and mouth. But he'd been wrong to suggest they'd reach for more, as she'd quickly pointed out to him.

"What do you mean?"

"I mean that maybe we've touched upon something special. Do you want to be with me again?"

"That wouldn't be wise."

"Why not?"

"Because as I said before, this is a small town and you're merely passing through, while I have to stay and live with the consequences. I can't afford an outright affair with you, Jake."

"I wasn't planning on standing in front of the post office and making a public announcement about it."

"Nevertheless, people see. They speculate. Believe me, I know."

"What about us then?"

"There is no 'us.'"

"I mean what about this? Is one night going to be enough for you?"

"It has to be. I meant what I said before, I wanted us to use each other and then go our separate ways. I still intend for that to happen."

As a result, he'd left—a little angry, more wounded than he was ready to deal with, and insulted. He'd dressed in silence and walked out, barely saying goodbye. For the first time—well, the first time since Jill's betrayal—experiencing having the tables turned on him.

Sure, common sense told him he was being a jerk. She'd only been holding to her conditions of the agreement. If he was smart, he'd accept that she'd done him a favor. The problem was he hadn't anticipated their lovemaking to affect him so.

With a groan he rolled over and pressed his face back into his pillow. His body stirred again as he remembered the honest passion they'd shared. When had he ever met anyone so direct and yet inexperienced as her? She'd begun as an enigma to him, one he'd been glad to tutor and watch evolve, bloom; the irony was, like a complex, multipetaled flower, she remained a mystery at her core and that intrigued him as much as her innocence had appealed to him.

He would never have believed anyone, let alone a virgin, could teach him anything new about gratification. Rain had proved him wrong with only one lesson: she'd taught him that it didn't necessarily have an end.

The ache in his loins intensified and he willed himself to focus on something else. Instead his mind conjured images of pale, firm breasts; he relived the hot, tight feeling of being buried deep inside her; he inhaled the beguiling, slightly musky scent of flowers and woman.

With a vicious curse, he pushed himself up off the bed and stomped naked to the refrigerator, not caring that all the drapes were drawn back. If she wanted a one-night fling, that's the way it would be, he told himself stubbornly. He needed a beer, that's all. Something wet and cool to help relax him so he could fall asleep.

But a glance in the near-empty refrigerator reminded him that he'd left the six-pack on Rain's coffee table.

"Crap," he growled, slamming the door shut. There would be no peace for him like this, and he knew there wouldn't be any cold water coming out of the shower taps anytime soon, either. With another choice expletive, he threw his body to the floor and began doing push-ups.

Rain awoke slowly, as though rising out of a dense fog. Even the morning sounds of birds and an occasional car, once she became aware of them, seemed muffled. It also took her a moment to realize her body ached, which happened the instant she dragged her spare pillow under her chin.

A low moan rose up her throat. It ended the second Jake's scent filled her nostrils and triggered her senses.

She opened her eyes. Remembered.

Oh, God.

So it hadn't been a dream. She'd done it. Not only had she thrown herself at him, he'd accepted. She'd slept with him.

Had sex with him.

She winced into the pillow, but knew there was no point in trying to sugarcoat it. Her decision had been made with a clear head. Well, almost clear, she amended, remembering that horrid postcard from Polly. Granted, Jake had pushed her to the edge, first with his audacious remarks and then with his body, but in the end the decision to give herself to him had been hers alone.

It was done with. She might as well be adult about it, and philosophical. There was nothing left to do but get on with her life.

But oh, she thought, rolling onto her back and gazing up at the milk-glass light fixture in the center of her ceiling, the experience had been indescribable. No matter what, she would always be grateful for his gentleness, especially when she'd momentarily lost her nerve and then hadn't known how to proceed. She'd heard stories about how it wasn't always pleasant for a woman the first time. From her new vantage point she believed the entire matter hinged on the sensitivity of the man.

Who would ever have thought Jake Marlowe would be sensitive?

She drew her arm down her body, and despite its achiness reveled as she recalled the way he'd touched her. Those had been caresses that had made a mockery of everything she'd ever experienced with Gil. If it wasn't for her levelheadedness, she might almost have believed they'd been worshipful; but, of course, she knew better than to let her imagination get too carried away. Nevertheless, she would cherish those moments for the rest of her life.

On impulse she slipped out of bed. Muscles and joints protested, but she stepped over to the closet mirror and considered the reflection of her nude body.

Did she look any different?

A faint hint of feverish pink still blossomed in her cheeks. Her hair had an attractive, tousled look that sleep alone had never yielded before, and her eyes ... Goodness, she thought, leaning closer to stare, her eyes were actually glowing this morning. They seemed enhanced with wisdom and mysterious lights.

Caught up in the moment, the abrupt but familiar sound of a bus gave her an unpleasant start and sent her heart thudding. There wasn't supposed to be a school bus driving around in the middle of July. That must mean ... she moaned silently. How could she forget? It was Sunday!

As with weekdays, her Sundays were also subject to a number of routines. Normally she attended adult Sunday school, then the regular service and afterward she liked to stay for the buffet luncheon, because it saved her from having to cook and eat alone.

But there was no way she could bring herself to do any of that today. Someone would only have to look at her and she knew a crimson flush would have them raising eyebrows and asking questions.

What's more, Gil and Polly were due back today. What if they made it in time for the morning service?

Crossing her arms over her breasts, Rain spun away from the mirror and headed toward the bathroom. She would plead an upset stomach or something. Considering that the thought of having to face those two made her feel queasy, it wouldn't be a complete lie. No, she needed a little time.

For the next hour she kept busy. After showering and
drying her hair, she prepared her breakfast. Then she
stripped the rumpled sheets from her bed and replaced
them with fresh ones. Next she decided to scrub down the
bathroom, followed by the kitchen floor once she'd convinced herself it was looking a bit lackluster, too.

She'd been about to carry the bucket of soapy water
out back when she heard a knocking up front. It sent her
pulse racing and she glanced at the stove clock.

Surely, it wasn't Gil and Polly, she reasoned. If they'd
made it back, they would be at church, along with practically everyone else in town. But what caused her heart
to suddenly begin pounding again was the realization of
who that left.

A slight shiver of apprehension raced through her.
What else did she and Jake have to say to one another?
There was always the option not to answer, of course, but
that would be taking the coward's way out. No, she decided, not after coming so far.

But as soon as she opened the door, she doubted the
wisdom of her decision. If Jake had been put out with her
when he left last night, his mood had since grown worse.

"I left my beer here last night," he said without pre-
amble, scowling at his boots.

"I know." She'd been cleaning around it all morning,
trying to decide what to do with the stuff. The notion to
carry it across the street had been rejected—not once, but
three times. Her concern was that she might give him the
wrong impression. "Wait a minute."

She crossed over to pick up what was left of the six-
pack, aware his gaze followed her every step. No doubt
he was wondering how he could have slept with her, she
thought, feeling more and more self-conscious. Well,
what did he think she should be wearing for a morning of

cleaning? The oversize shirt and loose shorts were utilitarian, and wearing her hair in a ponytail—hasty job that it had been—had seemed an improvement over her usual style. But he probably thought she looked like a frump again.

By the time she returned and unlatched the screen door, she wished she'd never answered his knock. She passed him his property without a word.

His scowl grew deeper. "It's warm."

"Of course it's warm. You left it on the coffee table."

"I know where I left it. But I thought you might have...never mind." His unfathomable gaze swept over her again. After a pause he asked, "How are you?"

"Fine."

"You sure? You didn't go to church."

"Sundays are my only day off. Chores pile up."

"Oh. Good. I thought maybe it was because of me."

Did he have to look so relieved to be let off the hook? "Hardly." She swallowed, feeling a tightness in her chest she suspected could easily become tears that she wouldn't be able to explain if her life depended on it.

Why hadn't he left well enough alone? A few more comments and questions and he was going to sound like a Monday morning quarterback. So help her, if he asked, *"Was it good for you, honey?"* she would ...

To her relief a car pulled into the station. "You have a customer," she said with a directive nod.

He didn't spare it a glance. "All right, I'll be honest with you. The real reason I came over was to ask if you wanted to do something later."

She let herself relish the invitation all of five seconds before firmly shaking her head. "No, Jake. That wouldn't be a good idea."

"We both have to eat. What's wrong with doing it together?"

"Why are you complicating things? I told you yesterday how I preferred to handle this."

"Dinner, Rain. I wasn't hustling you to get back in your bed."

Insulted by his crass choice of words, upset with his insistence in making this awkward for her, she did what she felt was her only prudent option. She slammed the door in his face.

Twenty-four hours later Jake continued to hear a ringing in his ears. It served well in aggravating his stung pride.

She had some nerve. He figured if anyone had a right to be hot, it was him. He'd tried to be solicitous . . . okay, after a somewhat bumpy start. But he'd gotten to the important things, such as asking how she felt and stuff, hadn't he? Nevertheless, she still wouldn't go out with him.

Who the heck did she think she was?

He understood her reluctance to get involved with someone who wouldn't be around for long. So be it. But all he'd been asking for was companionship. For some reason he was suddenly dreading the thought of having to face another frozen dinner and a night of TV.

The hell with it, he grumbled to himself. The hell with *her*.

"How ya doing, son?"

Caught up in his personal thoughts, Jake didn't hear Angus arrive until the man was almost behind him. "Spiffy," he muttered from under the hood of the sedan he was servicing. He saw no reason to pretty up his foul mood, even though Angus was technically his boss. He tossed the wrench he'd been working with back into the tool box beside him and reached for another.

"That don't sound convincing."

"Guess this heat is finally getting to me the way it is everyone else," he said, trying to be more sociable.

"I do understand that." Angus circled the car and settled an elbow on the opposite side of the hood. "Thought that shower the other day might improve things some, but it didn't last long enough, did it?"

Jake grunted. Not for some people, he thought sourly. It seemed the instant the rain had shut off, so had Rain's passion. "How's the arm?" he asked, more than ready to get his mind off her.

"Could be better," the older man replied, his expression forlorn. "Guess the humidity's what's making it ache so. My grandpappy used to get a crick in his neck whenever it got sultry like this. Suppose I'll end up with a similar condition. Can't say I understand how that doctor of mine is insisting he'll take my cast off by the middle of August."

It had been on the tip of Jake's tongue to ask if Angus might be ready to take back his job sooner than the six weeks Jake'd originally hired on for. But after hearing that remark, it seemed a useless question. Once again his spirits took a nosedive.

"Been hearing a lot of good things about your work," Angus continued, beaming at him.

"Thanks. I suppose that's better than complaints."

"Lots of people think I should hire you on permanent."

He straightened so fast he almost struck his head on the hood. "Oh, I don't think—"

"Hey, will you look who's here?"

Already rattled, Jake glanced around the sedan to eye the gleaming vehicle pulling into the station. The man and woman in the front seat weren't people he recognized and he looked to Angus to enlighten him.

"That's Rain's ex," his employer supplied conspiratorially. He gestured for Jake to follow him and headed for the car. "Hey, kids," he called. "Heard you got back. Jake, here's the only two folks left in town you haven't met yet."

Jake stopped in midstep. He didn't want to meet Gilbert Wakefield *or* his new bride. But short of being rude and neglecting his duties, he didn't see how he could get out of it. Snatching the rag tucked in his back pocket and wiping off his hands, he continued toward them.

In recent years first impressions had come to mean a great deal to him and this occasion proved no different. His initial impression of Wakefield made him want to pluck out the man's precisely trimmed mustache hairs one by one.

This was the man Rain had intended to marry? She might as well have fallen for a mannequin! Not that he wasn't handsome...in a passive sort of way. His black hair and mustache gave him a serious look, but his pale complexion and underdeveloped body made Jake guess he was used to spending most of his time behind the desk of that used car dealership he'd heard someone say he owned.

As for his bride, Jake concluded that it was irrelevant whether he was angry with Rain or not, Wakefield had opted for flash over substance. Polly Hansen-Wakefield matched her husband for outward prettiness with her short blond curls and dark blue eyes, but there was something calculating behind that flirtatiousness. The hint of sulkiness about her mouth wasn't an asset, either. Some might misconstrue it as a sexy pout, but having recognized it on Jill—too late, of course—he'd since categorized it as a mark of selfishness.

Glad to leave Angus to handle small talk, Jake went to the back of the car to pump gas. It provided him with a perfect view. One of the first things he noted was how Wakefield kept glancing across the street to Rain's house, even though the guy had to know she was at work.

Curious. Had the guy really cared for Rain? Jake had his doubts. Or maybe Wakefield was getting smart and recognizing he'd tied himself to a partnership with a boa constrictor who would squeeze the life and money out of him until there was nothing left. Maybe he was toying with the idea of seeking help from Rain.

Lots of luck, bud, he thought uncharitably. If he'd learned anything in the short time he'd known Rain Neelson it was that the lady had pride in spades. If Wakefield had gotten himself in a mess, he couldn't expect any sympathy from her. In fact she would likely chew him up like scrap metal and spit him out. What surprised Jake was the depth of pleasure the prospect brought him.

Once he finished filling the tank, he returned to the driver's window. "Plan on staying in town long?" Wakefield asked him, careful to keep his credit card out of reach as though Jake's answer depended on whether he was willing to pay or not.

Curious to know what he was up to, Jake offered an indifferent shrug. "Angus is the only one who can answer that."

"Considering the way business has picked up, I plan to do my best," the older man said.

Wakefield nodded and reached into the pocket of his starched short-sleeved dress shirt. He handed Jake a business card. "I have the auto dealership on the far side of town."

"Oh, yeah, the used car place. I know who you are," Jake drawled.

Something flickered in the other man's eyes and he again glanced toward Rain's house. "If there's anything I can do for you, let me know."

"Gil, honey, invite Jake to our party. We're having an open-house barbecue next week," Polly injected, leaning over her husband and presenting Jake and Angus with an eyeful of cleavage, courtesy of her low-cut T-shirt proclaiming His. "Promise you'll come? Say! I have a super idea—bring Rain! Poor darling could use a chance to get out of the house. She's such a homebody and workaholic. Have you met your neighbor yet, Jake?"

"I know Rain," he murmured, keeping his gaze on Wakefield. He was picking up signals he wasn't sure he liked, and also a challenge he was tempted to take on. "She has been kind of busy lately, but I'll check and see what she says," he heard himself add.

There would be time to call himself a jerk later...and to wonder why he felt the sudden compulsion to play white knight. Rain certainly wouldn't thank him for it, nor did she need him to make things sound as though they were more than acquaintances.

"Do that," Gilbert Wakefield told him, finally handing over the credit card. "Oh, and by the way, you are going to see to the windshield, aren't you...this being a full-service aisle and all?"

Jake couldn't resist. He grinned evily. "For an old friend of Rain's? Why not?"

He spent the rest of the day regretting that, instead, he hadn't used the squeegee to wipe Wakefield's smug smile

off his face. And to ponder what to do about the party
invitation. In a way, he resented the idea of going across
the street for what undoubtedly would be another rejec-
tion. But he should have thought of that before he'd let
Wakefield and his wife annoy him.

By early evening, however, his thoughts turned to
concern. What was keeping Rain? He'd already locked
up the garage and had retired to the trailer. Trying to ignore the sweltering heat, he'd stripped down to his jeans
and kicked back on the bed, planning to watch the only
station on TV that wasn't playing a ball game. When she
finally drove into the station about twenty minutes later,
her car sounded like an elephant with bunion problems.

Trying not to focus too much on his relief, Jake decided against pulling on his sweaty T-shirt or shoes.
Barefoot and beer in hand, he leapt off the top step of the
trailer and strode toward her, refusing to acknowledge the
sizzling cement.

Rain sat with her arms wrapped around the steering
wheel and her head resting upon them. Even her hair
looked tired, he thought, feeling his sympathies rising.
Several strands had escaped somehow from their fussy
arrangement and hung limply.

*Watch it, buster. You've got an ax to grind, remem-
ber?*

"Mmm-mmm. You are having one bad month, Miss
Rain," he drawled, not quite able to be totally sarcastic,
but not ready to fully forgive yet, either.

"What I'm having is a bad life." With a sigh she raised
her head and met his gaze through the open driver's
window.

Jake saw exhaustion, frustration and anxiety, as well.
Suddenly, he understood: she was expecting the worst
from him. She expected nothing less than retribution.

Like Saturday's flash storm, it quelled whatever impulse he'd had to get back at her.

He rounded the car to inspect the right front tire where a chunk of rubber had been torn out, then took a long swig of beer because he already knew he would soon be building up a powerful thirst. Taking his time, he returned to her side. "What did you do, run over a semi?"

"Only his muffler. There was no avoiding it."

"Whereabouts? I didn't see any truck passing in a while."

"Not in town, on the highway. I was in Oxford visiting old Mr. Herman, one of our senior citizens. He fell and broke his hip this morning. Being a widower with no other family, I thought he might be frightened or lonely stuck in a hospital."

"That was nice of you," Jake heard himself say.

Keep it up, Marlowe, you're going to turn into a real marshmallow.

"Not really. It's not as though I have any pressing..." Too late, she seemed to realize what she'd been about to say. She redirected her gaze to look out the windshield. "Do you, um, think I've done some major damage, broken the steering shaft or something? The car was shaking badly."

"It probably doesn't need anything more than a new tire and an alignment."

"Oh. Okay, then I guess I'll leave it here overnight and figure out another way to get to work in the morning."

She tried to avoid his silent scrutiny, but he didn't let her. When he failed to answer, she finally risked another glance at him.

"I mean, I know you're closed for the day."

"Are you asking me or telling me?"

A humorless smile barely lifted one corner of her naked mouth. He tried, but he couldn't forget how he'd been the one to remove all signs of her lipstick the evening they'd made love.

She drew a long breath. "I see. I'm going to be punished because I chose to stand firm on principle, is that it?"

"Excuse me for feeling I missed part of this conversation," he replied, tossing his empty beer can into the trash bin behind him. He shoved his hands into his pockets. To keep them from hauling her out of the car and doing ...

What?

"Lady," he said with a sigh. "You sure do spend an awful lot of time making assumptions as to what's going on in my head. And since when did I give you permission to speak for me?"

Rain gripped the steering wheel with a fierceness that made Jake think she wished it was his neck. "All right. You tell me what I'm supposed to say and how I'm supposed to act. After all, you have more experience at this sort of thing than I do."

"At what, messed up tires?" At her hard look, he shrugged. "Okay, for one thing, you could stop treating me as though you expect me to pounce on you at any minute."

"I am not doing that!"

"Sugar, you're more nervous now than you were before we did it."

Rain shut her eyes. "There's no need to go into extraneous detail. Maybe I'd hoped that we could politely step around each other for the duration of your time here, but this accident makes it clear that's not going to be a viable option."

"'Viable option'? Criminy H. Columbus, can the fifty-cent words, will you? We've got more than your momma's etiquette lessons to deal with, here."

"What do you mean?"

In as few words as possible, he told her about Gil and Polly's appearance at the station and Polly's subsequent invitation. As he'd expected, Rain exploded.

"You had no business sounding as though we're on those terms!"

"Hellfire, every time you look at me you turn red down to those cute little toes of yours. You might be able to fool some people around here, but how long do you think it would take before that sharp-eyed, she-cat of a friend figured out we were *intimate* strangers? And what new punishment do you think she'd make with the information?"

"Damn you, stop turning this into a crude joke!"

"Then stop trying to deny anything happened!" he yelled back.

His anger had the appropriate effect. She leaned back in her seat, seeming to take stock of how bizarre their conversation had become. "What made you tell her that you'd ask me to go with you, Jake? Why would you put yourself through it? Going there wouldn't be any fun. People would stare. Polly would gloat. I'd be miserable and therefore witchier than usual."

He leaned back against a steel pillar, his own exhausted temper leaving him feeling empty and inexplicably lonely. "The truth? I didn't like Wakefield's attitude," he admitted slowly. "Or Polly's. They're not nice people . . . and witchy or not, you deserve a break." He offered her a cautious, crooked smile. "You going to sue me for that?"

Her own expression gentled. "I couldn't afford the attorney fees." But her expression did grow somber. "I'm used to taking care of myself, Jake."

"Tell me something I don't know. What's wrong with living dangerously for once?"

"I thought I already had."

"Was it the worst experience of your life?"

He saw the blush rise to her cheeks, a deeper shade than usual. The doubt that had shadowed her eyes gave way to curiosity. "Why me?" she asked instead. "You must realize I'm nothing like the woman you took to bed. She was an aberration, born of a reckless moment. I don't intend to let her surface again, so you've been wasting your time if you've been thinking otherwise."

"Did anyone ever tell you that you think too much?"

She averted her gaze and shook her head. As tired as she looked, Jake decided she looked kissable, too.

"You're a bad boy, Jake. What's dangerous is that you like being bad."

"Sometimes," he admitted. For the right reason. For the right person. "But I'm the only one around who can keep you from getting beaten up emotionally by the Wakefields."

He leaned closer and rested both arms on her door. "Let's go to the party, Rain. If you don't show up, you'll never stop the whispers and rumors."

"If I show up with you, I'll be replacing them with new ones." Her voice took on the honeyed tones that tied his gut into a different kind of knot.

"Let people talk. Do you care?"

She considered that for several seconds. "One more question. What's in it for you?" she asked, and he knew by the resigned note in her voice that he'd won.

A slow grin spread across his face. "You mean the pleasure of your gracious company and a meal that doesn't come out of a microwave isn't enough?"

She whispered a word he would have bet a week's pay would never slip past her ladylike lips. It was delicately phrased and had him howling with delight. "Hot dog, you're on, Miss Rain. Pull up to that old garage door. I'm in a mood to wrestle with some rubber."

Six

───

"I'm warning you that if you do anything to embarrass me tonight, your life won't be worth whatever your disreputable motorcycle would bring as scrap metal," Rain muttered as Jake settled in behind the driver's seat of her car. She knew how that made her sound, but she couldn't help it. The man hadn't stopped grinning since she'd answered his knock at her front door, and her already-unraveling nerves weren't coping well.

"My, my... we are tense this evening."

She ignored him. "Your family will file a missing person's report. Rumor and speculation will flow rampant. But for all intent and purposes, you'll have disappeared off the face of the earth."

"All I said was that you looked as tempting as you did the night you wore that silky bit of nothing, and this is the thanks I get?" he replied innocently as he keyed the engine.

She couldn't help it. He had no appreciation of how she felt, let alone what she'd been going through.

After letting him talk her into going to Gil and Polly's "event"—as Polly had called it when she'd phoned Rain personally with an invitation—she'd taken a hard look into her closet and concluded that her wardrobe, like her life, needed a complete overhaul. One panic-filled shopping spree later and she was feeling the pangs of an imposter of the first order.

Her hands trembled as she smoothed the slim skirt of her blue-on-blue halter sundress. "You're right. But I'm feeling grim enough for the threat to stand."

Although Jake shook his head, his smile remained intact. He seemed in a rare mood tonight and that had influenced her caustic remark. Lethal enough when he wasn't laying on the charm, he'd almost had her staring like a starry-eyed girl when she'd first taken in his crisp black shirt and dress jeans. Tonight he exuded an aura of magnetism that left her mouth dry and her imagination replaying scenes from when he'd raced her to not one, but two, orgasms.

"Well, I hate to douse your bonfire, punk'n," he informed her dryly, "but it would take several personality transplants for 'the family' to care one way or another."

Too late Rain remembered he'd had no better luck in the happily-ever-after department than she had. She sighed and tried to make light of a bad gaff. "Go ahead, undermine my intent."

"Life's a rock, ain't it? You want to punish me? Let's drive to a secluded pasture. I'll spread my shirt on the grass, lay you down and you can show me what your breasts look like in the sunset."

"Jake!"

"Guess that's a 'no thanks,' huh?"

"Remarks like that are exactly what I've been talking about."

He reached across to caress her cheek with the backs of his fingers. "I'm trying to get you to relax and do that dress justice. Believe me, there isn't going to be a man at this shindig who won't be wishing he's the one who'll drive you home tonight. Besides," he added, again gripping the steering wheel with both hands, "instead of bickering, don't you think we should be getting our stories straight?"

"What stories?" She frowned, immediately suspicious.

"About our relationship."

"We're not supposed to have one, remember?"

"That was your plan, and initially a feasible one. But, honey, regardless of what you think you've been seeing in that bedroom mirror of yours, one look tonight and no one's going to believe I've kept my hands to myself these last two weeks. That is unless I'm—"

"Spare me."

"It's the truth."

"We're neighbors, okay? We're sociable," she added, ticking the details off on her fingers. "But that's as far as it's gone, because you're passing through town and not looking for long-term involvements."

"And you have a reputation to uphold."

"Exactly. Agreed?"

"Don't say I didn't warn you."

"*Agreed?*"

"Only under duress."

She refused to smile. She had her hands full as it was without encouraging him to be bad; he did fine on his own. Deep down, however, a tiny flame of excitement stirred, warming her. It proved to be her saving grace. He needn't know that he made her feel pretty; that's what she'd been seeing in her mirror lately. Tonight.

This evening she wore her hair in a casual flip, with only the sides held back by combs; and her dress truly was flattering, emphasizing her small waist and making her breasts appear more voluptuous than they were. Her doubts only returned when she tried to assimilate the Rain of old with this new phenomenon.

"Maybe you should tell me more about yourself," she suggested, willing to try anything to keep her thoughts off what lay ahead.

"What about me?"

She realized she had no idea where to start, and that she truly wanted to know anything he cared to share. "Where were you before you came to Stiles?"

"New Orleans."

"Oh."

He made a *tsking* sound. "Such disappointment to pack into one tiny word. Have you ever been there?"

"No, and I've never wanted to go, either."

"Why not? It's a wickedly fun place."

"My point exactly."

"Great restaurants."

"You went for the *food?*"

He chuckled, and she hated that his smile sent a wave of seductive warmth across her skin like melted butter. "Touché. Great music, too, and... ambience."

"If I was you I'd stop while I was ahead."

His deeper laugh, as laden with innuendo as the heavy air flowing in through the rolled-down windows, heightened her awareness of her body's feverish state. "Before that I was on the Texas coast, working as a hand on one of the deep-sea fishing boats, and the summer before that I spent in California."

"Let me guess, L.A.?"

"Palm Springs."

She struggled to think of what quixotic job he'd taken on there. "Golf caddy?"

"Bartender."

"You *have* been around. Don't tell Gil that one or he'll draft you to flip off the tabs on beer cans the rest of the night."

"No one can make you do or be something without your permission."

His serious tone drew Rain's gaze. She studied his profile, so strong and determined in the amber light of early evening. "Do you honestly believe that?"

"I hear a note of objection. Are you going to tell me that Rain Neelson is a product of accidents? Is it missed opportunities or circumstances out of your control that's brought you to where you are today?"

Why did he have to make it sound like poor motivation in an old B-grade movie? "Life intrudes, Jake. I went to school at the University of Mississippi at Oxford because it was necessary to stay close to home. My mother was never strong health-wise. With my father often being away from home—"

"Why?"

"Excuse me?"

"Why was he gone? Did they have marital problems?"

"No! I... Every marriage has a few ups and downs. What I meant to point out is that my father sold insurance and his territory was huge."

"What did your mother think of his being away so much?"

Rain turned to look out her window in time to see another farmer disking under his heat-ruined crop. The acres of brown earth looked sterile compared to the green promise they'd held back in spring. It struck her that her parents' relationship had ended up just as lifeless despite their initial feelings for one another. But she couldn't admit that to Jake; it would feel like a betrayal, even after all these years. Especially after trying not to dwell on it herself. "What is this?" she said with an uncomfortable laugh. "Twenty questions?"

"I'll bet your mother was lonely," Jake continued, as though she hadn't spoken. "I'll bet she tried to make your father feel guilty sometimes."

"She had a difficult time coping. She was beautiful and she'd been very popular as a girl." Rain had heard the stories about her many beaux and the parties and the proposals countless times. "She simply wasn't made for the life she got," she insisted, also trying to forget the way she used to stop listening once her mother started rambling on and on for the third or fourth time in a day.

"Then why didn't she do something about it?"

Rain sighed, the same old impatience growing. "I told you, she was vulnerable. She was always catching some bug or another."

"Was she too ill to leave your father and make another life for herself?"

"She would never have left him. She loved him!" Rain cried, aghast that he could suggest anything of the kind. There had been a bond between her parents; it was just...complicated. "A woman's role as wife and mother was so different during my mother's time. And what you have to understand is that the Southern woman has always been in a position of playing catch-up to women from other parts of the country."

"So she used you to fill those big blocks of time while your father was away to entertain her and care for her."

"She was my mother! How could I have done otherwise?"

"By demanding that she stop living in a fantasy world," Jake shot back. "Choices, Rain. The same type of choice that convinced you to underplay your looks so you wouldn't have to compete with hers."

Rain went rigid in her seat. The car grew unbearably hot. "You think you're ready to hang out a shingle and add psychiatry to all those other trades you've taken on, don't you?" she snapped, her voice scathing. "But you missed one important detail. When I was twenty-one my father was killed in a convenience store robbery gone bad. Granted, he left us with some insurance, but Mother could never have survived on her own. She had no marketable skills even if she was strong enough to work, and my father's death had upset her health terribly."

"I'm sorry. I didn't know about your father."

"No, you didn't. You probably heard some gossip about his long absences from home and made some snappy conclusions." Hurt and indignation pumping painfully through her veins, she held on to her clutch purse with the same desperation that she tried to restrain her temper. "Even if you were right in that I did alter some of my dreams to adjust to what life handed me, at least I dealt with my responsibilities and didn't run away from my problems."

"Are you suggesting I did?" Jake asked quietly. "Okay. What was my responsibility, Rain? To stay on a ranch that would never be mine and watch my brother and the woman I'd loved play duke and duchess of the county? That's what my mother thought I should do because tradition demanded blood sticks with blood. Well, I'm not wholly against tradition, but I don't buy into the theory that I'm bound to participate in it after it's kicked me in the teeth.''

''And you never go back?''

''For what?''

''They're your family.''

''Honey, the winter after California I met an old man living in the woods of East Texas with a three-legged dog, two raccoons and a bullet from Korea that was finally burrowing into his spinal column. I stayed with him for almost a year. I tilled his few acres of bottomland, I cooked his meals and I cleaned up after him when things got so bad he couldn't even crawl to the bathroom. And in the end I held him in my arms and let him think I was the son he'd lost in Vietnam. He wasn't a blood relation, but he was more *family* than anyone I'd ever known before or since.''

They arrived at the only four-way stop in town and, raw-voiced, Rain gave him instructions to make a left turn. For a long while they were the only words between them.

It had surprised her to hear him speak so vehemently, not only because it contradicted the laid-back, easygoing personality he usually tried to exude, but because it spoke of scars not yet healed. What troubled her was how it also threatened to affect the arm's-length relationship she hoped to maintain between them from here on out. She couldn't afford to care, not about a man like Jake who'd had all the illusions shaken out of him for longer than she had.

And yet her heart ached for the unhappiness he'd known. And for the way he tried to deal with it.

''Guess I ticked you off good, didn't I?'' he asked, slowing as they approached the long line of cars that signaled they'd about arrived at their destination.

Rain considered the vehicles parked on either side of the street near the house she'd once believed would be her home. "No. Actually, I was thinking how this exchange emphasized our incompatibility. I have a history of sticking around no matter how hard things get and you follow some other principle."

"I guess we are pretty different," Jake replied slowly. "But that doesn't mean we can't get along."

"Enough to stop hurting each other?"

His long look was a physical caress. "I don't know why I nearly went rabid on you," he said, his voice gruff.

She nodded, understanding the impulse as well as the regret. "If we've learned anything in the past five minutes, it's that we're both walking wounded. Maybe it bothered you to recognize that. Maybe your lecture was directed more at yourself than it was at me, I don't know. What I do know is that I'd prefer us to be allies rather than enemies."

Once Jake made a three-point turn and parked behind a pickup truck, he shut off the engine and shifted in his seat to face her. "You've got yourself a deal under one condition," he murmured, skimming a finger across her bare shoulder.

"What's that?" she asked, aware her throat was going dry again.

"Trust my instincts on how to play this."

He didn't exactly make it a request, but rather a somber demand, his dark eyes boring deep and neutralizing her defenses. "That all depends," she replied, more cautious than ever.

"Stick close to me as much as possible. Follow my lead even if you think I'm pushing things, and most of all, don't let anyone turn you into a victim."

She tried to read what he was up to in his expression, but his calm, craggy features gave little away. "You don't strike me as a man interested in becoming a Svengali."

"I'm not. But," he added, an intimate, teasing light returning to his eyes, "I am the man you gave your virginity to."

Yes, and in doing so he'd shown her how reality could be ever so much more sensual than her fantasies. But that didn't mean she was ready to give him carte blanche to direct her life. "We'd better get moving," she said evasively. "We're already fashionably late."

With a deftness she was beginning to understand was intrinsic, Jake came around to open her door. "You want to make it look authentic?" he asked as he took her hand in assistance. Her expression must have mirrored her mixture of confusion and suspicion because wicked laughter lit his eyes even more. "Kiss-swollen lips," he explained. "Passion-glazed eyes."

Before she could veto the idea, he slipped his hands around her waist and tugged her against him. It was then she saw the determination and fierceness he'd camouflaged with teasing. Her heart began pounding, her body grew aware and hot.

"Don't you think that would be overkill?" she managed, squeezing her hands between them and against his chest. She discovered his heartbeat wasn't any calmer than hers. "The fact that we're here together should be enough to send tongues wagging and assure Gil and Polly I'm not falling apart over their deception."

"Trust me," he replied, an instant before taking her mouth with his.

She tasted mint and man, absorbing the energy that vibrated beneath her palms and from his hard thighs pressing against hers. Before she knew it, he made her oblivious to their surroundings, she forgot that she was supposed to be unexciting, abandoned Rain Neelson. All she knew was that either he was the world's most superb actor, or he truly wanted her. What woman was strong enough to resist that?

Captivated by the moment, the dream, Rain slipped her arms around his neck and gave herself up to the desires he triggered in her. Just once more, she told herself, for moral support. Dutch courage. Gratitude . . .

"Now you two stop putting on that shameless display. The whole neighborhood's bound to be watching!"

Jake recognized the singsong voice of Polly Wakefield and tightened his hold on Rain, whose sudden stiffening told him she wanted nothing less than to break their connection like a guilty schoolgirl caught necking on her family's front porch. "Easy does it, honeybun," he whispered, giving a loving nip to her ear. "Use the moment." He needed one himself to get his raging hormones under control. God, the woman could kiss.

"You saw her coming, didn't you?"

He could tell by the tension in her body, as well as her voice, that she was recovering far faster then he was. "I plead the Fifth." He lifted his head and offered both Polly and a stunned-faced Gil a sheepish smile. "Sorry, folks. Guess you caught us."

"Well, I don't have to ask why you're late," Polly continued, her deep blue eyes darting back and forth between him and Rain with what he could easily read was curiosity and skepticism. "Rain, you sly dog. You didn't tell me you two were an item."

Although he hugged his wife more closely to his side, Wakefield's face didn't quite relax into a sincere smile. "I don't think it's any of our business, Polly. Rain . . .

Marlowe. We're glad you could make it. Rain, you look lovely."

"Yes, I was about to compliment you myself," Polly gushed, her own smile bright but empty. "Gil's promised me an entirely new wardrobe, so you'll have to tell me where you found that darling outfit. I wonder if they have any in a smaller size? Our Rain is always finding things she insists would look better on me," she explained to Jake.

Before he could tell the pretty shrew she would have a hard time holding a candle to the woman he held with discreet firmness at his side, Rain replied, "Oh, not this time, Polly. I'm afraid the hips run narrow with this design."

Jake wanted to throw back his head and howl and he could have kissed her. He settled for a subtle squeeze of her waist.

But he knew as surprised as Polly was, she had more experience at being witchy and covered it well. Drawing away from her husband, she took Rain's arm. "Never mind. Gil prefers me in silk over cotton anyway. Now, you come along with me. I need to get another tray of goodies from the fridge—I swear these people are eating like it's their last supper. Anyway, it'll give us a chance for some girl talk. You gentlemen will manage without us for a few minutes, won't you?"

Jake considered blocking her maneuver, but he caught Rain's silent look of entreaty and acknowledged that perhaps it was best to let her try a few moments on her own. "All right, but don't try and introduce her to anyone else," he warned. Then he avoided Rain's glare by adding to their host "What's to drink, Gil? My blood sure could use something to cool it down."

While Jake usually avoided stirring up trouble when dealing with people, it gave him considerable satisfaction to watch Rain's ex go through various degrees of annoyance, curiosity and growing unease. What got confusing was his own motives.

He told himself he was giving the shorter man a hard time simply to pay him back for hurting Rain. To a degree that was true; as he'd told her, taking her virginity had left him feeling somewhat responsible for her. But after about an hour of suffering Wakefield's company, he came to the conclusion that he was also doing it for himself.

Gil reminded him of his brother. Maybe not in looks, but in attitude. Like Jack, Gil had grown up to be self-possessed, if not outright selfish. Jake decided it was a pleasure not only to show Wakefield that Rain had survived his desertion, but that beneath her no-nonsense veneer lived an exciting, sensual woman.

However, that still didn't explain the restlessness he felt whenever she was out of sight, or the odd feeling of possessiveness he experienced when he watched her display of affection for someone who stopped her to talk. If he didn't know better, he might believe he was falling in love. But he figured he was too jaded for that. It had to be simply lust and typical male territorial instincts, he told himself as he mingled with the crowd. Whatever it was, he continued to keep one eye on Rain.

Practically half the town seemed to be here and one of the picnic tables on the patio was heaped with pastel-wrapped presents. Jake recalled how Rain had wanted to bring a gift, too, but he'd insisted she rethink the matter, or at least wait and choose a more private moment. "You don't reward someone for pushing you out of a plane without a parachute," he'd told her.

When he spotted Angus and his wife, he went over to visit with them. The enthusiastic party-goer used the opportunity to introduce him to several people he hadn't yet met and it was reassuring to note that by and large Rain's fellow residents were a friendly lot. But primarily, as promised, he kept close track of his date.

"Don't you think it's time you ask me to dance?" he drawled, once he caught up with her again. He liked how merely an innocent suggestion could turn her cheeks a permanent shade of delightful pink.

"I thought it was the gentleman who invites the lady."

"But as we both know, I'm no gentleman." He did, however, draw her into his arms.

"The designated dance area is over there," Rain said, nodding to the patio lit by tall candle torches where several couples were moving lazily to a bluesy country-western tape.

"Too crowded." He lowered his cheek to hers. "Also too bright. This is far more cozy."

"People are staring."

"They have been all evening. It's because we make an intriguing couple. If it bothers you, close your eyes and I'll take your mind off it by whispering sweet nothings in your ear."

He felt rather than heard her brief, reluctant laugh. "I wish I was as good at this as you are. Flirting, I mean."

Jake felt a twinge of hurt that she hadn't considered taking him seriously, but quickly pushed it away. "You have a talent for something far more important," he murmured, stroking his thumb across her smooth, bare back. "Sincerity can be far more potent."

When he felt her step falter, he raised his head and saw she wasn't even paying attention to him. What kept him from being exasperated was noting the look of hopelessness on her face and where her attention was focused. Following her glance, he eyed the stiff-shouldered man in the plaid Western-style shirt and dress jeans. He was leaning against a tree out of reach of the colorful lanterns stretched around the yard, and doing his best to gulp down a long-necked bottle of beer. "Who's that?" he asked.

"George Gibbons. He was my competition for the postmaster's job."

"Ah." Jake met the man's glare and held it. "He's still holding a grudge after all this time?"

"I guess so. All I did was ask where his wife, Nancy, was tonight and he told me to mind my own business."

"Maybe they had a fight and she went home without him."

"Nancy?" Rain uttered a sound of disbelief. "She makes *me* look like a hard-nosed feminist. She and George married the day they graduated from high school and she's barely been out of the kitchen since, except to give birth to their three boys."

"On second thought, maybe she was too exhausted to even make an appearance." Jake ducked his head to brush a kiss on Rain's shoulder. The immediate shiver that raced through her slender body pleased him, until she stopped dancing to look up at him.

"I've had enough of this pretense. Do you think we could leave?"

Again he felt a stab, and again he told himself it was ridiculous. They'd made their point to Wakefield and Polly. In fact, he could see Rain's ex standing with the mayor and the school principal and good old Gil still couldn't seem to keep his eyes off her.

A flash of heat lightning stretched across the indigo sky and he glanced upward. He couldn't help but remember the last time it had rained. It filled him with a strange yearning as well as a hunger to taste that passion again. "Yeah," he muttered, "I guess I've had enough, too. Looks like everyone will be leaving shortly."

"The lightning won't amount to anything."

Before he could reply, he spotted Gil, who'd left his group and was headed toward them. "Don't panic, but our illustrious host is about to descend. Hello, Wakefield. Going to yield to the weather and send us home?"

"Actually, I thought I'd ask Rain for a dance."

"I don't think—" Rain began.

"I don't think—" Jake said at the same moment.

They stared at each other. For a moment Wakefield didn't exist. A breeze flirted with the lush leaves on the oak tree towering above them. Another flash of lightning lit the sky and tension was a palpable, breathing entity closing in on them.

Just then Polly emerged from the house and uttered a shrill cry. "This can't happen to me! Gil? Honey? What do we do?"

Jake saw Rain start, blink at Polly and finally relax. "I—I'd better help her put a few things inside."

As soon as she was out of earshot, Jake met Gil's unabashed look of disapproval. "Don't ask for what you can't handle, Wakefield."

"I'm sure I have no idea what you're talking about."

"And I'm sure you're smarter than you look."

"Now see here, Marlowe—"

"No, you listen," Jake replied, keeping his voice low and his smile easy. Only his eyes, if anyone looked close enough to tell, reflected how deadly serious he was. "You had your chance, but you weren't smart enough to realize what you had in Rain. Now it's my turn . . . and, mister, the one thing I don't do is share. So back off."

"Regardless of what's happened between us, I still consider Rain a friend," Gil declared stiffly. "Nothing you can say will change that."

"Lucky for her, I'm around to teach her that friends like you are as useful as rattlesnakes."

"Well, it's clear her taste in companionship has gone downhill lately." Wakefield added his own more glib smile. "Don't threaten me, Marlowe. Rain has always put history before everything else, and I've known her forever."

Jake wanted nothing more than to rearrange the pompous jerk's over-pretty face. "Mister, I don't threaten. I promise." Brushing him out of the way, he went to save Rain from her other headache.

"Come on, Polly, make the most of the situation," Rain said, picking up another colorful tray and loading it with paper items that a spontaneous shower would ruin. "I'll help you start organizing things inside and then you'll be prepared no matter what happens."

Although her former best friend followed with another load, she seemed more interested in posing and pouting. "It's not fair. I've been planning this party all week!"

"That long? My word, and to think I believed all our farmers watching their crops frying in the fields had it rough," Rain replied drolly. She nudged the screen door open with her hip and brought the first batch of items to the kitchen table. Sometimes, she fumed, Polly's self-centeredness was barely tolerable.

"You're usually more sympathetic, Rain."

"What can I say? It's been a full week."

"I knew it." Polly set her tray on the counter and whirled around to face her, her gypsy dress's handkerchief skirt flaring around her shapely legs. "I'd hoped your agreeing to come tonight meant you'd reconciled yourself to Gil marrying me."

"Oh, Polly." Fatigue washed over Rain like the waft of steamy air breezing in through the screened door and windows. "I'm really not in the mood for this."

"But we need to clear the air. I still consider you my very best friend in the entire world."

Rain stared at the innocent-eyed woman before her and wondered how she could ever have been so foolish as to believe Polly's act. "You *must* be joking."

"I know Gil and I hurt you. But is it our fault we grew attracted to one another?"

"Whose fault was it then?"

"It just...happened."

"And that makes sneaking behind my back all right?"

"Rain, honey, what you need to focus on is that you and Gil would never have been happy anyway."

"You're right. Whereas I'm a stickler for fidelity, he's a two-timing louse. Thanks for clarifying that for me."

Polly rolled her eyes and set her hands on her round hips. "I wouldn't throw stones, honey. After all, every-one here tonight is wondering what you're doing with a man like Jake Marlowe."

"I beg your pardon?" Rain was beginning to find their entire conversation absurd. Granted, she'd had a hunch Polly might try to gloss over what she and Gil had done, but to lecture her about Jake? "I'm not about to discuss my private affairs with you."

"You don't have to. I can see you're throwing your-self at the man because you're on the rebound."

"*Throwing myself?*"

"Sure, hon. I mean, look at you. Granted, you look kind of nice and all in that color," Polly said quickly, "but that's simply too much dress for sweet old you. And then there's the small matter of that man not being the reliable sort, if you know what I mean? Why, Rain, he even gave me one of those come hither smiles of his, and here I am with the ink barely dry on my marriage license!"

"Mmm . . . but the question is, is there even a marriage license?" Rain drawled.

Polly stared at her. "What?"

Rain didn't know what she felt like doing more, laughing hysterically or giving Polly a long-overdue slap. "Why am I only now beginning to see how priceless you are? I'll admit there's not much I am sure of these days, but one thing for certain is that if anyone was doing any flirting it was you. That's how you tricked Gil into thinking you cared about him and how you got him to marry you. What you're too immature to realize is that marriage takes a lot more work if you're going to make a success of it."

The sweet smile slipped from her former friend's carefully penciled lips. "I can see you're in no shape to listen to helpful advice," Polly said tightly.

"Helpful? Always. Nonsense? Never. Thank you for an . . . educational evening. I think Jake and I will be going now. Sorry to leave you with such a mess to clean up. On the other hand, it'll be good practice for you. I have a feeling you'll be finding yourself knee-deep in it before long."

Seven

"**V**ery impressive."

Rain was grateful for the steadying support of Jake's arm around her waist as they descended the porch stairs together. She'd had no idea he'd been coming to get her and had been standing at the screen door. Taking possession of the purse he'd collected for her, she whispered back, "Tell me you didn't hear everything?"

"Enough to feel confident you won't be used as a doormat again."

For a moment they were waylaid by people wanting to say a few final words, but finally they were following the shrub-lined walk to the street. Adrenaline continued to surge through Rain. "I can't believe her nerve. Polly's always been a flirt and self-centered, but to want to hurt me that way." She shook her head, incapable of finding the words to describe her feelings, or those that would explain the woman.

"It was bound to happen. You committed the unforgivable."

She frowned. "I don't know what you mean."

"You didn't fall apart. You aren't pining for gorgeous Gil. You've definitely ruined her fun," Jake concluded, accepting the keys she drew out of her purse and offered to him.

Rain considered that while he unlocked the passenger door for her. "That's a profile of a very unstable person."

"Nah. Very human. She's into one-upmanship." Once Rain was settled, he closed the door, then circled to the driver's side. "How was the evening all in all? Rougher than what you'd expected?" he asked, locking his seat belt.

Lightning brightened the sky from indigo to pink and violet, illuminating clouds and suggesting a shower might follow after all. Rain watched and reflected. "Surprisingly, no. I think I'm more angry than hurt. Does that make me cold-blooded?"

"That makes you smart."

She shot him a suddenly shy smile. "I owe you most of the credit for that. You were wonderful."

"I was, wasn't I?"

They laughed jointly and he started the car. Soon the Wakefield residence was behind them and in the distance the wind-tossed four-way stoplight bobbed like a buoy in a stormy sea. Rain rolled down her window and breathed in the turbulent night air, not caring what the wind did to her coiffure.

"Tired?"

"A little." She stretched, scooped her hair up off her neck and sighed before relaxing back into her seat. "Actually, I feel as though a huge weight's been lifted off my shoulders, so there's more relief than fatigue. But heat or no heat, I bet I sleep like a baby for the first time since this whole fiasco began."

"Atta girl."

They drove in companionable silence for a while. Rain gave herself up to the hot caress of the wind. In a way it reminded her of the night Jake had taught her how it felt to be a woman, when he'd skimmed his talented hands over her body until she'd thought she would burn up with need and hunger.

By the time they passed the post office, her stockings felt unbearable. She hadn't wanted to wear them in the first place, but she'd been raised to believe a lady suffered for etiquette.

She shifted in the seat. The combination of internal and external heat was making her stick to the vinyl. As she parted the neckline of her halter dress to the sultry wind, she closed her eyes and transported herself to the town lake. How wonderful it would be to strip and jump in for a luxurious swim. Of course, that wasn't going to happen. Barely a week ago Norm had told her about seeing a water moccasin in there as big around as his arm and twice as long.

An unexpected and huge drop of rain splattered against her chest. With a gasp, she jerked upright and saw several more droplets scattered across the windshield. Not enough, however, to turn on the wipers.

"Feels good, doesn't it?"

Slowly rubbing the droplets into her thirsty skin, she glanced at him. He had his left hand out the window, taking his own personal inventory, but he must have glanced over and seen what she was doing—and how much of herself she'd been exposing.

How strange. A few weeks ago she could never have sat here so comfortably around a man. Not that she was feeling all that comfortable. Jake was too physical a presence, too virile to take for granted in any way.

He pulled into her driveway during another flash of sheet lightning that illuminated their surroundings beyond what the amber porch light did. Shutting off the engine, he turned to her. "If it starts pouring, what do you say we play tag out there and the winner gets to lick the loser dry?"

Leave it to him to keep her imagination vivid. With a helpless laugh, Rain climbed out of the car, hearing him do the same. "I don't think so." As she came over to his side, the first lazy rumbling of the night thunder echoed in the distance. "Besides," she said, holding out her hand for her keys, "it's not going to do more than raise our hopes."

"It's done that," he murmured.

But when he failed to pass over her keys, and instead tugged at her hand, it struck Rain that he hadn't been referring to the weather. "Jake," she warned gently.

"I haven't done anything."

"Yet."

With a beseeching smile, he leaned back against the car, looped his arms around her waist and drew her between his spread legs. "C'mon. Stay with me for a few more minutes. It's not that late."

"It's not the hour that concerns me." It was the growing sexual awareness between them. After an evening of frequent touches, discreet though they might have seemed to people watching them, she could tell Jake had been left as deeply affected as she'd been. But she resisted the slight pressure at the small of her back that would have brought their bodies into full contact. "You're not going to be bad, are you?"

"Maybe a teensy bit?" His grin narrowed his eyes into wicked slits.

Rain looked away in order not to let him see her amusement. He was getting too adept at undermining her defenses. "This isn't fair. You promised to behave."

"One kiss and then I'll condemn myself to that tin oven across the street and my lonely, lumpy matchbox of a bed."

"Not a good idea."

"I haven't earned one circumspect kiss?"

At the word circumspect she lifted her left eyebrow; she also shifted her purse between them like a shield. It did nothing to repel his masculinity, but then she hadn't been expecting miracles.

Jake studied her expression for a moment and the humor and teasing vanished, replaced by a wry grimace and . . . a touch of regret? "You're getting to read me too well."

"I'm sorry." He was that much more lethal when he let his gentle side show. "Believe me, I *am* grateful for what you did tonight."

"I want you, Rain."

So much for trying to tiptoe around their physical attraction time bomb. How could it be this powerful? The mystery of intimacy was already behind them; it should have subdued things. But no, every word, every minute, made it worse.

She shook her head sadly. "I can't."

"You mean you won't."

"It's the same thing."

"You want me. You want me as much as I want you."

He began massaging her back, his hands moving slowly upward from her waist to bare skin. He was slow in his exploration, thorough, as though he couldn't stop, or else was in no hurry to move on. Rain couldn't help but stare at him. "Yes," she admitted, "but I also know I can't risk being with you again."

He frowned. "Is it because . . . I took care of precautions last time."

"I didn't mean that," she replied, her embarrassment tempered by the longing he stirred in her. "I meant . . . I suppose what they say about men and women being more than physically different is true. Men can be casual about . . . sex. It's harder for a woman than I'd believed. At least it is for me."

He didn't answer. Rain decided words would be redundant; she could tell by the sudden lack of emotion in his face that he understood what she'd been driving at. Even though he didn't remove his hands, didn't physically withdraw at all, it distressed her, and she felt an irrepressible need to explain.

"You needn't worry," she began, not quite able to meet his steady gaze. "I'm not so naive as to think I've fallen in love with you. But I'm smart enough to know that I can't take the risk that I would if this went any further. And, no, it's not because you're a drifter. That has less to do with it than I'd previously thought.

"You're an angry man, Jake," she continued with a bravado she credited to the energy pulsating around them. "Oh, you hide it well with wit and sarcasm, but it's there under the surface. And I don't think you like women much—or maybe it's that you don't trust them, I haven't figured out yet which is which. Whatever the case, I'm not about to get caught up in it . . . or you. I spent most of my life struggling to make things work, to make people like me, love me. But I always ended up giving more than I got in return. I'm through with being emotionally shortchanged.''

Jake shifted his hands up her sides, higher until the backs of his fingers brushed the curves of her breasts. ''I wouldn't leave you unsatisfied.''

Rain didn't know whether it was his touch, his gruff voice or an abrupt drop in the temperature, but she shivered. ''No. What you'd do is leave me wanting more, but you *would* leave.''

Jake mouthed something—a curse, she was sure of it—and released her. The loss of his touch made her feel empty and heartsick. When he abruptly spun around and buried his face in his folded arms on the roof of her car, she had the strongest urge to wrap her arms around his waist, hold on tight and swear she'd been wrong, didn't mean it, wanted him to forgive her. But it would be a mistake. Even for an experience as exciting and unforgettable as Jake Marlowe, it would be a mistake.

Not knowing what else to do or say, she started for the house.

''Hey.''

She whirled around. He stood in the same place—except that he was holding up her keys. Shaken, she retraced her steps. Just when she could actually feel the man-warmed metal caress her palm, he shifted his hold and lifted her hand to his lips.

In the space of seconds she felt everything—his breath, his teeth, his tongue. His passion took all the oxygen out of the air and she thought she might collapse from the shocking starkness of it.

And then he was walking away, merging with the night, a man she didn't understand and couldn't keep. She closed her fingers tight around the keys, wishing it were possible.

The metal's bite mocked her as devastatingly as Jake had tempted her.

"Where'd you learn how to do that?"

Jake glanced up from the old golf cart he'd been repairing, to Norm Uttley and then at Angus. He wasn't sure the wide-eyed man wasn't pulling his leg. Deciding Norm probably didn't know much about electricity in general, and wiring in particular, he shrugged and replied, "Can't recall. Here and there. Were you serious when you said this was for your wife when she checks on the kids?"

"Yeah. We got three boys on seventy acres. Sometimes it can be a handful trying to track 'em down."

"Guess so." Jake wiped the back of his hand across his sweaty brow to cover his grin. He had to admit, though, it was nice of the guy to try to make life easier for his wife. Showed he cared about his boys, too.

There were a lot of decent folks like Rain's rural carrier around here. Unique, but unpretentious. It had been a refreshing discovery after getting to know the Wakefields. But nice as people were, it was beginning to look as though he needed to vamoose.

Angus didn't want to hear anything about it. Jake had tried several times now, but as far as the old-timer was concerned he still owed him another three weeks on their verbal contract.

How could he make him understand without explaining too many details? He had to come up with something; things were getting too complicated. No way could he last another three weeks with Rain across the street and him in his borrowed prison. The mere thought of her set off an ache that by night spread through his body, making sleep impossible.

He wanted her. He'd tried not to, but she'd given him a taste of something he'd never expected to find again. Unfortunately, she'd also pegged him right; he'd been caught up in his anger too long. Rain deserved better than to get involved with him; she deserved a chance to find a man who had more to offer, and so he intended to do the right thing, move on before they got any closer, before he hurt her.

"That should about do it." He closed the Fiberglas covering the cart's engine. "Let's get this back onto your trailer and you'll be set to go."

He and Norm rolled the vehicle out of the garage and up the two boards they'd used as a ramp. While he helped the man secure it with rope, Angus went inside the store to get them some soft drinks to offset the baking sun's debilitating effect.

"It wouldn't hurt to get a couple bricks locked in behind those tires," Jake told him, slightly winded. "You don't want to take any chances going around country-road turns. Angus has some stacked at the back. I'll go get them."

His thoughts wandered, thanks to the heat...and Rain. Actually the two were almost synonymous these days, which also explained why he was nearly at the tumbling stack before a shadow to his right caught his attention. He turned...and saw smoke far back in the field. Before he could convince himself the dreaded was happening, horrific flames climbed high into the sky.

Fear momentarily froze him. What lunatic had started it? Didn't they know that as dry as things were around here it could wipe out this entire area if the wind picked up?

He spotted two kids on bicycles chasing toward the shacks.

"Hey!" He waved his arms high over his head and the older one, the kid who wasn't crying, spotted him. "What's going on?"

The boy made a sharp turn and raced toward him. His explanation was equally frantic. "You got a shovel, mister?"

A shovel wasn't going to help, nor five nor even twenty-five. The waist-high growth, gone mostly to weed, was a feast vulnerable to starving flames like those. All anyone could hope for was containment so that more than brush wouldn't get devoured.

"Is there anyone else back there?" Jake demanded.

The boy's dark eyes were huge in his dust- and sweat-tracked face, reflecting fear with an honesty only a child's could. His coffee brown, short-cropped hair glistened with sweat from heat and exertion. "My brother and Ricky Perez, they're throwin' dirt on the fire, but alls they got is they hands. Please, mister, can you help?"

"Get on home and start warning people in those houses," Jake told him, pointing to the vulnerable buildings on the south side of the field. "I'll call for help and then get your brother and friend."

Without waiting to see if the boy did as he'd been told, Jake raced back to the front of the garage. "Angus," he yelled. "Call the fire department! The field's on fire. Unhook your truck from that trailer, Norm. We've gotta get some kids out of trouble."

"Who-wee, will you look at that."

Malva's declaration and the fire engine siren brought Rain hurrying from the back. She joined the woman and George at the front counter in time to see Stiles's one truck race past, followed by a police car. Two volunteer fire fighters soon brought up the rear in their personal vehicles with their flashers on.

"Where're they going?" George asked Cy Moore, the owner of the café who'd hurried into the building. Cy was also the cook, and had a police radio in his kitchen to offset the boredom of standing over a sizzling griddle twelve or more hours a day.

"Field fire behind Angus's garage." Cy's short-sleeved white shirt was limp with sweat and an odor of smoked meat and fried onions followed him into the building. "That's across from your place, ain't it, Rain?"

She nodded, worried. "Did you hear how bad it was?"

"Nope. But I'm sure the boys'll get it. Anyway, don't fret none. Angus's pumps'd have to blow first, and them alone'd wipe out half a mile of stuff."

"Gee, Cy," Rain moaned, "that makes me feel so much better."

The man laughed and asked George for a money order. Despite a strong urge to race home and check on things herself—and Jake—Rain forced herself to return to the supply room and double-check the inventory of their stock. If her home was in jeopardy, someone would let her know, she assured herself. As for Jake...he was an adult and could take care of himself. Besides, she'd made it clear days ago that there was no future in involving herself with him.

But for hours afterward, she kept one ear tuned toward any news a customer might bring. When the ambulance that Stiles shared with the neighboring community of Pottersville raced through town a half hour later, her heart plummeted along with her spirits. Could it be for Jake?

It was inevitable that her thoughts stayed around him. These days it seemed impossible not to think about the man since a bittersweet melancholia was underscoring their relationship. *Relationship?* She shook her head for being so presumptuous. You had to consciously make attempts to see a person to have a relationship. Talk. Reach for an understanding. Yes, they remained polite, even friendly, when their paths crossed; nevertheless, they were doing their best to stay away from each other.

But dear God let him be all right, she prayed. Naturally she wanted everyone out there to be safe. Most of all she was restless to go there and see for herself. She was trying to justify a way to do that when Norm, who was on vacation this week, wandered into the building. Once she realized he'd been at Angus's and she heard Jake's name, she stopped pretending to be busy and came out to hear clearly.

"...so after I unhitched the trailer we drove back there to get the other kids out. But the wind had picked up and the fire was spreading. The kids were trapped. Jake told me to go back and get the fire extinguishers. Then he snatched up the tarpaulin I keep in the back and jumped out. That guy's a crazy man, I tell you."

"How bad was he hurt?" Bud Cox asked, still carrying the empty delivery boxes he'd walked in with after finishing his own route.

"Jake's hurt?" Rain heard herself gasp. When the whole group eyed her with various degrees of curiosity and surprise, she decided she could care less. She needed to know. "What's happened, Norm?"

"He burned his left hand some, but I guess you'd have to say falling on a busted bottle hurt more. His left shoulder needed about sixteen stitches. But he's okay."

"Okay?" Rain felt her temper getting the best of her. "They don't send out the ambulance for nothing!"

"That was for one of the boys' mom. Shana Jones. She heard her son was caught in the fire and she fainted. Being she's several months pregnant, they thought they'd better get her in for observation. They wanted to take Jake, too, but he wouldn't go. Angus finally talked him into letting us carry him over to Doc Brownlee's."

For the rest of the day Rain dealt with a restless anxiety to get home—or rather, to get to Jake's and see for herself how he was doing. Instead she tolerated Bud's lengthy phone calls, although she knew they were from his latest girlfriend. She even refrained from raising an eyebrow when George muttered he had to leave early and walked out, without actually getting her approval. There were simply more important things on her mind.

By the time it was finally her turn to leave, she'd made a few phone calls herself. After locking up she went across the street and picked up two fresh apple pies from the café and a whole meat loaf with the trimmings.

She delivered one of the pies and the meat loaf dinner to the family whose mother had been admitted to the hospital for overnight observation. Although shy, the grandmother and children were eager to tear into the various boxes and bags Rain presented. She left glad she'd thought of the idea.

Her route had taken her straight past the garage and she'd noticed it was already closed. Now as she returned, she found that anything but reassuring. It meant that Jake must be feeling terrible. Once she pulled into her driveway, she could hear the sound of the TV coming from the open windows of the trailer. Good, she decided, hopefully he was lying down and taking care of himself.

The scent of smoke still hung heavily in the air. The blackened expanse of field got her attention, too. The fire had gotten dangerously close to several buildings, including the garage. It made her all the more grateful things had turned out as well as they had.

She hurried inside and changed into one of her new outfits, a soft tank dress in a wisteria print. After that, she rushed to the kitchen and used the microwave to defrost two steaks, bake a couple of potatoes and add it to the large dinner salad she'd picked up at the café. All that was stacked in a wicker basket, along with various items she thought she might need. Finally she was ready to go across the street.

He didn't respond to her initial knock. She wondered if he'd fallen asleep, or could he be hurt more seriously than Norm had said? Deciding she wasn't leaving until she knew, she checked the door. It was unlocked.

"Jake?"

She stepped up and into the trailer. Almost simultaneously there was a bump and a rude expletive from the bathroom. Rain shoved the basket on the dinette table and hurried down the hall. "Jake?"

He didn't answer right away. Finally there came a reluctant, "Rain?"

No, not reluctant, she amended, strained. She was convinced he'd hurt himself. "Let me in?"

"It's not locked."

He sounded exhausted. When she opened the door and peered through the steam, she saw why.

He was holding his bandaged shoulder and was hunched over, obviously in pain. From the amount of water on the tile floor, she could imagine what had happened. "Oh, Jake. Why?" A sigh underlined her sympathy. "You know you aren't supposed to get stitches wet."

"I was trying not to, that's why I fell," he ground out through clenched teeth. He grimaced when she continued to stare at him. "Don't look at me like that. If you saw how filthy I was, there'd be no way you'd want me to crawl into a clean bed either."

"Sheets can be washed," she replied, primly. "But what I think really happened is that you lost your balance and fell while trying to put on your shorts," she added, nodding to his white briefs, which were his only attire.

With a shake of her head, she opened the door the rest of the way and turned on the overhead fan to get the steam out of the room. Then she checked the cabinet and drew out three towels. Each was spread across the floor to sop up the spreading puddle.

"So much for my irresistible body," Jake grumbled.

If he only knew, Rain thought. It was hard not to cast yearning glances over the various parts of his anatomy she was all too knowledgeable about, but fortunately her concern for his safety allowed her to concentrate on other matters and toss back, "You're in no shape to think about sex."

Her dry but gentle scolding earned her a snort. "Honey, I plan to think about it until the day they plant me." Then his voice took on a wistful tone. "Rain...you shouldn't be doing all that. I can get it—ouch, damn it—later."

Rain kept her touch gentle but firm as she brushed away his restraining hand and pushed him back against the wall. "You'll be sleeping later."

It was all she could do to resist slipping her arms around his waist and smothering him with kisses, she was so relieved to see his wounds weren't more severe. Instead she backed away and focused on examining the two bottles of pills the doctor had prescribed. "Have you taken either of these yet?"

"No. I had a beer instead."

"Very smart."

"I don't like pills."

Because she resisted taking them herself, she let the matter drop for the moment. "Are you in a lot of pain?"

"Yeah. You want to know where?"

"I'm serious." Despite the wicked gleam in his eyes, she kept her own expression somber.

"I'll live."

"Uh-huh. I think you'd better lie down. Can you walk to the living room or do you need my help?"

Jake's frown grew into a scowl. "What did Norm do, drop me off and race straight over to report to you?"

She fought back a smile and slipped an arm around his waist. "Naturally. Haven't you heard that men really are worse gossips than women?"

Once she got him settled on the narrow bed, she had an opportunity to examine his hand. Even with the protective bandages covering the medicated creams she could see streaks of angry red. "Dear God," she whispered. She couldn't help it; her heart wrenched at the sight of his injuries. Instinctively, she began to reach for it, but quickly withdrew.

"Hey," he teased gruffly. "It's all right. The shoulder hurts more."

"Everyone is talking about how brave you are. You saved those boys' lives and our homes...."

"The fire department helped some." But dry wit aside, he seemed to bask in her praise. "Were you really worried about me?"

The husky caress in his voice sliced straight through her defenses and probed deeply into her heart. "Yes." However, the realization didn't please her, no more than it had when she'd learned he was unafraid of danger. Bad enough that she would never forget him; she now had the additional worry that he would end up getting himself killed during some future act of bravery.

"Rain..."

She spun away from him and began unpacking her basket. "Look what I brought. I decided to save you from having to eat another frozen dinner." By the time she got down to the apple pie it was already filling the room with a delicious aroma.

"I'm too hungry to scold you for bothering," he admitted with a sheepish smile.

He also appeared relieved that she'd brought enough for two and planned to join him. When he used the remote control to shut off the TV, she decided it was because talking worked better to keep his mind off his pain.

"How was your day?" he asked.

Rain familiarized herself with the kitchen before putting their steaks in the broiler. "Busy, but hardly as eventful as yours. With Norm being on vacation and George handling his route, that leaves us shorthanded inside."

"George was the guy with the attitude problem at the party, right?"

"That's him." But she didn't want George to ruin her time with Jake. "Tell me who's going to mind the business while you're healing?" she asked instead. "Has Angus thought of that?"

"He's got a left hand that works and I've got a right. We've decided to form one unit."

Rain couldn't see how he hoped to have the strength to get out of bed tomorrow, let alone work, and told him as much.

"We'll manage."

In other words it was none of her business. Hurt, she concentrated on topping their potatoes with cheese and sliding them into the microwave.

"Speaking of the party..." Jake said after the silence between them began to lengthen.

"We weren't discussing the party."

"Humor me. Have you heard anything from the Wakefields lately?"

She shrugged. "Not really."

"That means you have."

He was certainly being persistent, she brooded. "Gil came by on Monday to apologize for Polly. Knowing her, she must have told him what happened herself."

"And? Your expression tells me there's more to it than that, Rain. He's been back since, hasn't he?"

"A few times." She pretended to hunt for plates to divide up the salad.

"Leave it in its tray," Jake suggested. "We'll share." When she hesitated, he added more quietly, "Isn't it a little late to worry about either of us being contagious?"

The temperature in the trailer rose at least ten degrees, and it had nothing to do with the weather or the broiling steaks. Rain turned around and stared. "What are you doing? Why are you sounding accusatory?"

"Maybe I don't like Wakefield hanging around you."

Jealousy? From Jake? Rain didn't know whether she felt flattered or indignant. "He's not 'hanging around me' and even if he was it's none of your business."

"If not mine, then whose?" he snapped, coming off the bed with a speed that stunned her considering his condition. When he slipped his right arm around her waist and drew her against him, she pressed her hands against his bare chest.

"Jake, your stitches—"

"I don't give a damn about them. Why are you opening yourself up to getting hurt again? I thought you were over the guy."

Flattered by the look of concern on his face and grateful that he cared at least a little, Rain sighed and touched his cheek. "I am. But I can't very well deny him access to the post office."

He shut his eyes briefly before lowering his head so that their foreheads touched. "Rain... God. Forget the steaks and stuff. Lie down with me. Let me hold you. Let me..."

She could feel him swelling against her and it only served to intensify her own yearning. "We can't."

"I swear I won't ask for more. I just want to feel your body against mine." He turned his head and, brushing a kiss into her palm, slid one of his own down to her wrist and then, with a muffled groan, he pressed closer and sought her mouth.

Although she wanted nothing more than to meet his hungry lips, take this stolen moment, she knew it would only be inviting more heartbreak. "No, Jake. Please? Neither of us deserves this."

He went still and for several seconds Rain could feel him fighting his body. But she was totally unprepared when he dropped his hands to his sides and ground out, "Everything's got to be on your terms, doesn't it?"

His anger and rebuke struck her like a shock wave. She stepped back, unable to believe what she'd heard, unable to think of anything to say. When he turned away from her and looked out the kitchen window, she could only stand there and stare at the way the long, lean muscles of his back stayed tense and knotted.

"I, um, just remembered something I needed to do back at the house," she murmured, finally collecting herself. "Do you think you can manage the rest of this on your own?"

"Sure."

"There's not much left to do. The steaks should be ready in five minutes and—"

"Whatever. I'll handle it."

His brisk voice convinced her to give up. "Okay, I guess I'd better go then. Take . . . take care of yourself."

"Rain?"

She was at the door, but she couldn't bring herself to look at him. If she did, she was afraid she might burst into tears. "Yes?"

"I've decided to leave."

Oddly enough it was exactly what she expected him to say. So why did her legs suddenly feel like undercooked egg whites and her stomach turn as though she'd eaten something indigestible?

"When?" she managed to ask.

"As soon as I'm sure these stitches won't rip open too easily. I'm telling Angus tomorrow."

Eight

―――

"I'm telling Angus..."

Rain glanced at the clock on the other side of the service counter. It was nearing two in the afternoon. By now Jake had told Angus. Would he try to change Jake's mind? Would he succeed?

"I need to take off for the rest of the afternoon."

Rain glanced over her shoulder at George and frowned. "You can't be serious? This is the second time this week."

"It can't be helped."

His words were barely audible and behind his glasses, his eyes shifted left, right, everywhere but at her. She sighed and shook her head. "You'll have to do better than that."

His answering look had her wondering if she'd pushed too hard. If he did walk out, she couldn't let it matter; he owed her some explanation. Yet when he clenched his hands into fists, she steeled herself for the worst.

Suddenly his shoulders slumped and he hung his head. "Can we do it in your office?"

Rain asked Malva, who was filling tomorrow's bulk mail into rental-box slots, to monitor the service counter for a few minutes. In her office, she closed the door and thanked George. "Despite what you may think, I'm not the enemy," she added, hoping her friendly tone would relax him and gain his trust. "So, what's up?"

There was still reluctance in his demeanor. "I was trying to keep this quiet."

"Whatever you tell me, it won't go past this office," she assured him. "You have my word."

That seemed to placate him somewhat and, after a deep breath, he said, "As you probably know, my son attends the Green Mountain Military Academy north of here. A few weeks ago, he...he was caught trying to steal a test."

"Oh, how heartbreaking for you. George, I'm so sorry."

He dismissed that with an impatient gesture. "It shouldn't have been a surprise. I'm pushing, always pushing, trying to make him into the achiever I never was. The pressure got to him."

"Has he been expelled?"

"Not yet. He was offered another chance due to his previous academic and disciplinary record. But there are conditions. One is that our family takes a certain amount of counseling each week."

Which explained why he'd been so edgy, and also why he'd been leaving early. Rain crossed her arms to keep herself from reaching out and offering sympathy. It would take time before George was ready for that much friendship from her. But she intended to let him know she cared.

"Thank you for telling me. And by all means take the rest of the afternoon off. I'll work with you to get through this. You needn't worry any longer."

His expression reflected shock and doubt. "Just like that?"

"Why not? I asked a question. You told me the truth."

He ran a hand over his thinning hair and cleared his throat. "That's... What I mean is... Thanks. Thanks a lot. I guess I haven't been very fair to you. I hope... I want you to know I appreciate this."

"I can see that, and I'm glad." *Well, what do you know,* she added to herself. *Miracles do happen.*

But not all miracles were timely—or welcome. A few hours after George left, Gil walked in. Rain wasn't overly surprised to see him. Although they had talked since the party—usually when he'd carry over boxes of bulk mail advertising his current "specials"—it hadn't been often or for long. They'd both seemed to have grown more awkward around each other.

This afternoon, however, he was empty-handed. Rain watched him run a hand over his salon-styled hair, and noted the walk that was self-conscious compared to Jake's loose-hipped stroll. Amazing, she thought. Whatever hurt Gil had caused her, she had honestly gotten past it and him.

"You know there was a time I thought you'd never smile at me like that again?"

Realizing he'd misunderstood, she kept her greeting polite but impersonal. "How are you today, Gil? Is it my imagination or are the clouds building up outside from more than afternoon heating?"

"The radio weatherman says there's a chance of a shower. But I hope not. I just had the cars polished for my weekend sale."

"We need the rain, Gil," she chided softly. "Customers wouldn't mind a watermark or two."

He shrugged that off before smiling more warmly. "You look like a spring rose today."

A few months, even weeks ago, she would have been thrilled to hear such a compliment; now it troubled her. She'd had positive feedback regarding her new, more feminine wardrobe and looser, flattering hairstyle. But it was one thing to be told by old Mr. Herman that she was "a nice-looking little chicken" and another to be praised by Gil. Lowering her eyes, she brushed away some nonexistent lint from her dusty-pink dress. "Thank you," she murmured. "What can I do for you this afternoon?"

He glanced around. Rain was tempted to tell him that George had left hours ago and that, with Malva in the back, they were virtually alone. But he beat her to it. "I need to talk to you privately. Could we go into your office?"

"I'm sorry. I need to stay here until closing time. We're a bit shorthanded," she added, then was annoyed at herself for explaining too much. She didn't want to be impolite, but she didn't owe Gil Wakefield any explanations, either.

For the first time she caught a hint of some inner tension in him. Rain had no idea what to expect, but something told her that with her own headaches these past weeks and Jake's decision to leave sooner than originally planned, she wasn't in the mood for any more surprises.

"Then what would you say," he began quietly as he leaned closer, "if I came over after you got off from work?"

"You mean to the house?"

He nodded.

There was only one thing to say. "Why?"

"We need to talk."

"You have a wife for that," she reminded him.

Gil touched his tie and glanced around again. "Rain, you don't understand. The reason I want to see you is to explain. I think... I think I may have made a serious mistake."

"About?"

"Polly."

She didn't know what to say. It didn't help that she felt the strongest urge to laugh. This had to be the most astounding, ridiculous thing she'd heard in ages, not to mention insulting. Why tell her? What was she supposed to do?

"You don't believe me," he said, his tone wounded.

"I don't understand you," she said, curling her fingers into fists until her short nails bit into her palms. "People don't go through the trouble of having a clandestine relationship, elope and then within a week of their honeymoon decide it was all a mistake. At least not outside of Hollywood," she amended dryly.

Gil drew himself to his full five feet ten inches. "I'm aware that you have every right to say, 'I told you so,' but it would mean a lot to me if you didn't. I'm here to ask you to meet with me, work with me. Wait for me. I realize now that Polly and I are all wrong for each other. I'll admit she's attractive and sexy, but... she's going to bankrupt me within a year at the rate she's spending my money."

This time Rain didn't bother trying to hide her feelings. Mirth had her mouth twitching from laughter. "I see. You're in the market for a cheaper model?" she asked, amused by the comparison Gil inevitably made between a life partner and his precious automobiles.

"No, of course not. But...well, *you* would never have demanded I scrap virtually everything in my house and start from scratch. You wouldn't ask for the most expensive sports car on the lot simply because I happen to own the dealership. And...Rain, she doesn't want children!"

That last declaration caused her a stronger twinge. Thanks to Gil and Polly, she knew her own plans for a family had been put on hold, perhaps permanently. "She's only twenty-five," she reminded him.

"But *I'm* thirty. I want a family while I'm young enough to enjoy them." He shook his head. "I should never have let you go."

"You didn't. You're the one who left."

His face lit with hope. "And I want to come back."

"Oh, brother."

They were her thoughts, but it wasn't her voice she heard speaking them. Rain turned to see Malva outside her office, holding a report she'd been working on. "Er, on my desk will be fine, Malva, thank you." She turned back to Gil. "I'm sorry."

"I knew this wouldn't be the right place for this. Let me come over later?"

"That's impossible."

"Why? You don't have other plans?"

She wished she could say she did. "No. You do. You're going home to your wife." As far as she was concerned that was all that needed to be said.

But Gil seemed to have other ideas. "It's Marlowe, isn't it? He's taken my place."

"Jake's leaving town shortly."

"Oh." Gil mulled over that revelation for a moment and then leaned across the counter to take hold of her hand. "I won't say I'm not glad to hear it. I won't lie to you."

"That'll be a novelty," Malva muttered, reemerging from Rain's office. Her laceless sneakers made a shuffling noise as she dragged her feet while heading to the back.

This time Rain couldn't quite restrain all her amusement. In the last few weeks she and Malva had shared some interesting conversations. She was growing to enjoy the other woman's dry wit and practical thinking. She also appreciated her loyalty. But Gil was a problem she had to deal with herself.

"Thanks for finishing that for me, Malva," she called after her. "Why don't you start getting your things together, we'll be locking up in a few minutes."

She turned back to Gil. Her expression was neither apologetic nor encouraging. His own reflected disbelief, but also determination.

"We'll talk again," he said.

"I hope not. Not about this. It's over, Gil."

"You don't mean that. You love me."

"I wanted to believe I did," she replied, trying to be as kind as she could. "Now I'm not so sure. What I *am* certain of is that I won't settle for less than the real thing next time." Her thoughts inevitably shifted to Jake. "I want a man who thinks I'm exciting and who finds himself breaking his own rules because he wants me."

"Marlowe," Gil murmured.

Rain chose to neither deny nor agree. But she knew her silence was incriminating.

"I won't take no for an answer," Gil told her, his old confidence returning. "I suppose I'll just have to show you I mean business."

While she'd never dreamed she was the type to rouse jealousy in a man, Rain could take no pleasure out of Gil's change of heart. In fact, his declaration depressed her.

His words echoed in her mind as she climbed into her car, adding to her general state of melancholia. It was bad enough that Jake's leaving would start tongues wagging and fingers pointing her way again. If Gil really did separate from Polly, would he insist on involving her?

Like the apocalyptic overtones of the weather, Rain's spirit weighed heavy on her. Above, the sky had turned into a solid slate gray cover of clouds. The air grew thick and breathing difficult. When she spotted the huge splatters of rain staining her jumper-style dress, the same that now pelted her car, her eyes flooded. There was something she had in common with her mother; she'd always thought rain was good crying weather.

Still she fought back the tears, deciding the skies would have to weep for her. She couldn't let down her guard until Jake was gone. It would be humiliating to let him know that she couldn't hold up to her own dictums. But her heart was breaking.

She would miss him so. He must never know the truth, but she'd fallen in love with him.

By the time she was around the bend, the droplets became a downpour. She turned on her windshield wipers and tried to focus on what gratifying news this would be to area farmers, the reservoirs and the earth in general.

She listed all the things she could, should do inside since it would be impossible for any yard work. Finally, she made it to her house and parked in her driveway, ready to congratulate herself for redirecting her thoughts away from Jake. Then she made the mistake of glancing in her rearview mirror.

All pretenses deserted her. She didn't give two cents whether or not it was raining. There was Jake, locking up the garage for the day. Possibly for the last time.

Hardly aware of what she was doing she grappled with her seat belt and stepped out of the car.

Jake stopped.

As the heavens bequeathed them with a gully washer, they stared at each other through the liquid veil.

Common sense told her to go inside.

Why? another voice asked. *You're already soaked.*

But she was behaving like the kind of woman she'd always vowed she would never become.

What—honest?

Honesty wasn't always a virtue.

As though the two sides of herself had merged, she felt a deep wrenching pain. Just once more, she thought, watching the rain sleek his hair and mold his T-shirt and jeans to his lean but powerful body. She wanted one more memory with him.

She pressed the lock on her door and slammed it, securing her purse in her car. Keys gripped in her hand, she began walking, then running...across the street...across the garage's potholed driveway, to the man who remained motionless. Watching.

She stopped before him. They stared at one another, the rain so loud it silenced the world. Rain gripped her keys harder, willing him to give her a sign to let her know that this was his choice, too.

His eyes were narrowed against the pelting rain, shielding his thoughts from her. And then, as though he couldn't help himself, he touched her cheek. Tenderly. Cautiously. With such care, she felt it to her bones and in her blood. It filled her with such relief and joy, the world around her spun dizzily out of focus.

She closed her eyes for a moment and absorbed the feel of him, leaned her head into his touch to hold it a second longer. When he shifted his thumb to stroke her lower lip, there was no holding back the strangled cry that rose from her heart.

Did she reach for him or did he pull her close? She didn't know. All she knew was that suddenly they were together. His mouth seeking hers, then moving restlessly in a deep, searching kiss she prayed would never end. Caution gave way to hunger and then to desperation. They couldn't seem to capture the moment fast enough, thoroughly enough, and yet they tried. They tried.

He jerked his head back. She heard a roaring in her ears and a sound that could have been her name but common sense told her was most likely the rain. She didn't want to deal with logic nor wisdom tonight, not questions, nor doubts. All he needed to know was that she wanted him and unless he'd suddenly gone blind he would see that in her eyes.

He saw. When she touched his lips, he grasped her hand, pressed a kiss into her palm and licked the rain sluicing down her fingers. Then he suckled the spot where her pulse was pounding madly before stepping backward and drawing her with him.

The mechanics were lost to her, she could have floated up the stairs or even walked through the door like some spiritual being, but somehow they made it inside the trailer. The slamming door echoed the thundering of her heart. She didn't know what she did with her keys, either. One moment they were clutched tight, the next both of her hands were free and she was reaching for him.

It happened again—the speed, the abandon. He pulled her close, tight, and found her mouth with a marksman's precision. This time he branded her. His. Forever. It was in the possessive stroke of his tongue and in the fierce way he ran his hands over her body. When he wanted her to give him more of her mouth, he grasped a handful of her hair and drew her head back until her breaths became gasps. She let him. When he backed her against the refrigerator and sandwiched her between it and his own equally hard length, she encouraged him. All the while his hands explored and demanded, coming to rest finally on her hips and urging them deeper into the hard center of his.

"Can't get close enough," he groaned, against her lips. "Can't get enough."

There was something unbelievably erotic about the wetness of their clothes plastering against their bodies like second and third skins, also from the heat they built from their passion. There should have been steam rolling off them. Maybe there was. Neither of them stopped to look.

When he sought the sleek, damp column of her throat, she arched her neck to give him free access, but there was no stopping her shiver as his hands drew down the zipper of her dress and the cool wall of metal touched her desire-heated skin. His hands moved to her front, briefly skimming over her breasts and back up to slide the dress off her shoulders. It spawned more heat, more need.

Her bra was one of the new items of lingerie she'd purchased recently. His brief but sizzling inspection of the sheer scrap of pastel lace convinced her every penny was well spent. An instant later he built on the simmering mood between them by starting a trail of hot and moist kisses over every inch of skin he exposed.

When his steamy breath warmed the upper swell of her breasts, she bit back a moan and gripped his waist in expectation. But haste no longer seemed a priority for Jake. Rather than cover her with his mouth as he had done the first time, he cupped her with his hands and buried his face in the shallow valley between.

"You smell like rain and flowers." He stroked his thumbs over her nipples until they grew so hard, even the restraint of delicate lace hurt.

"Jake . . . please." The caresses were torment enough, but the faint stubble of his afternoon beard added a wicked variation.

"I will, for as long as you like," he replied, deftly unsnapping the front closure of her bra. Then that scrap of material, too, fell away. "Then for as long as *I* like."

Rain shut her eyes tight and pressed her head back against cold steel, absorbing the sweet agony of Jake's mouth on her. His lips wet, his tongue laved, shooting her to another level of sensual frenzy. Desperate to touch him as he was touching her, she wrestled with his T-shirt, bunching it up inch by inch until he sank to his knees, allowing her to drag it over his head.

"Your bandage—" she gasped, momentarily having forgotten.

"Never mind. I don't."

She wanted him to stand again. She wanted to hold him, press herself against his hot body, but he had his own plans. Almost fierce in his concentration, he slid her dress and slip down over her hips until they fell, puddling around her feet. It left her in nothing more than her new lace-topped pantyhose, and she wondered how he would take that.

He didn't disappoint. The slow upward journey of his gaze was coupled with the equally languid slide of his hands from ankle to calf. He paused to kiss the outer side of her left knee and then continued up the back of her thighs, at which point he leaned forward and nuzzled the triangle of taupe lace that was all that separated her from him.

"Lady, lady," he whispered hoarsely, "if I knew this was all you were wearing, I wouldn't let you out in public."

Then he opened his mouth over her and the wave of shock and pleasure that crashed through her had her knees buckling, her breath locking in her throat. Jake responded with a low chuckle, but he didn't stop. Belying yesterday's injury, his strong hands held her in place.

It was torture, it was bliss. Rain wanted him to never stop, but she wanted to be a part of him more. Finally, she grasped his hair and forced him to meet her gaze. "Let me touch you, too," she pleaded.

The fire in his eyes told her what her request meant to him. With the grace she found as arousing as his body, he rose and she drew him close. It felt unbelievably wicked yet wonderful. Their bare skin, her sleek hose, his wet jeans. Their mouths sought a kiss and they pressed closer and closer.

Outside the downpour grew heavier. It was a silent rain, as though all its energy was focused on one thing. Rain understood that kind of concentration. She felt it for Jake, wanting him in any way, every way she could have him.

It was her idea to reach for his belt, and she could tell the move surprised him. But he adjusted fast, letting her ease him back just enough to get her hand between their bodies. She wasn't as quick or talented as he was and it made her self-conscious. He must have sensed it; suddenly, he caught her hand and drew it inches lower, to the rigidness beneath the zipper.

"This is because of you. Don't doubt yourself with me. Ever."

Ever. As if there would be more than this last time. Awareness that there wouldn't gave her the confidence to return to focusing on his belt and then the snap and zipper. Sometime in the midst of it all he began kissing her again and the next thing she realized he'd maneuvered them to the bed.

It was his look of blatant arousal that gave her the courage to slip out of her heels and lower herself to the narrow mattress. As she reclined in silent invitation, her heart pounded so hard her chest ached. Did it show she was afraid, afraid of making a fool of herself? she wondered. Afraid she would grow so damp he would be turned off?

Her doubts vanished as she watched Jake strip with the same casualness she'd come to know was intrinsic to the man. He also took her breath away as he had the first time she'd seen him naked. A moment later he was with her on the rumpled sheets, seeking her lips and molding her body to his.

"You're so hot," he whispered against her temple. "I've never known a woman who looked at me and caught fire as you do."

"It's easy with you."

"Talk like that to a man like me can get you into trouble."

"I hope so."

The intent in his eyes grew ever more determined and he drew his hand down her body. "Then we'd better get you comfortable."

He kept her gaze trapped by his as he slid his uninjured hand from her throat to between her breasts to the waistband of her sexy hose. "If I live to be an old . . . old man," he drawled, brushing kisses on the skin he exposed as he drew the waistband downward, "I'll never forget how sexy you look at this moment."

Because it sounded too much like a goodbye and she didn't want to think about that, she closed her eyes and concentrated on the way his hands felt against her. Even the gauze covering his left palm felt unbelievably seductive against her sensitized skin. She gave herself up to the moment, although deep inside her heart ached so that tears burned in the backs of her eyes.

He was too sharp to fool. Suddenly he was looming over her and demanding, "What is it?"

"Nothing. I—I don't want the rain to stop, that's all."

He was silent a moment, as though he couldn't figure out what she meant or if it was the truth. The silence deepened, lengthened. Then, abruptly, he reached over her head and into the drawer of the side table. In the next instant she was doused with a waterfall of small foil packets.

"What are you . . . ?"

He plucked one up and began ripping it open. "I picked these up the day after we made love. I wanted to be prepared in case you got in the mood to seduce me again."

She might have believed he was teasing her, until she saw the pulsebeat at his right temple. That small token of vulnerability was enough to convince her not to be shy when he took her hand and showed her what to do.

"I don't want the rain to stop either," he rasped, his gaze holding hers. She tightened her fingers around him, and every feature grew taut, as though he was on the edge of some incredible agony or pleasure. "But if it does, I'll go turn on the shower."

"No." Rain shifted her hand around his neck and drew him down to her. "I will."

Somehow their kisses changed. They were every bit as passionate as before, but now they regained the intimate quality they'd had that other evening once the walls of self-consciousness and doubt had toppled. Then Jake slid his hand between them and began touching her as she was touching him and there was only need. Hot, humid need.

She urged him closer. He found his place and slid into her with an intentness she found thrilling, filling her, filling her until they both gasped.

"Oh, my...Jake."

"Damn you feel good. Damn...it...all...to..."

"Don't swear so much."

"Don't..." he groaned and his movements grew fiercer "...tempt me so much."

She bit her lower lip, but it was impossible to hold back a moan. Already he was threatening to make her lose control. Then she was there and nothing mattered but holding tight as ecstasy claimed him, too.

They were silent a long time afterward. Still together, but only because the bed was too small. Rain told herself that, while secretly wishing it was because Jake couldn't bear to leave her yet. Whatever the reason she was glad. If this was to be the end, she wanted to prolong it.

But finally the suspense was too much for her. "Did you tell him?" she asked softly.

Nine

___

She thought he would never answer. It was obvious he'd heard her; she felt his body stiffen, an emotional withdrawal.

"Yeah," he said, after an endless waiting.

"When?"

"Tomorrow." He rolled off the bed and disappeared into the bathroom.

Rain stared up at the pressboard tile ceiling. *Don't cry. Don't you dare cry.* But she wanted to. As she listened to water run and compete with the continuing shower outside, she struggled with the burning in her eyes, the sharp knifelike pain in her throat and the ache in her chest. Out of desperation, because suddenly even breathing became a chore, she sat up.

It had been a stupid question. Of course he'd told Angus he was leaving tomorrow. There was nothing for him here. What they'd shared certainly wasn't enough, was it?

She looked across the room and for the first time noticed his duffel bag on one of the kitchen benches. It was open and several items were stacked on the table. He'd already started packing.

Rain turned to the window and shifted the curtain. It was raining so hard, water poured off the trailer's roof, creating a solid wall, obliterating her view of the rest of the world. It occurred to her that he probably wouldn't leave as long as the weather held. Childish and selfish impulse though it might be, she secretly wished it to continue raining—knowing it wouldn't.

How was she going to survive without him? She hadn't wanted to fall in love; a part of her still wanted to deny she had. But the emotions churning inside her were too strong to disregard or mislabel. She'd fallen in love with a drifter, and tomorrow he would ride out of her life as casually as he had come into it.

She smiled as she thought of their first encounter. He'd terrified her, annoyed her, but ultimately he'd intrigued her. How wrong she'd been about him. They'd misjudged each other.

And tomorrow he would become a part of the past.

She had to be brave. Let him go with a smile. She'd always loathed weak, clinging women. Besides, it wasn't as though he would be leaving her entirely. Not even *he* could take her memories away from her.

Jake rested his hands on the bathroom sink and stared at his reflection in the medicine cabinet's mirror. It was always dark in here because the window was small, and with the weather it seemed later, almost like dusk. Yet he didn't bother with a light. Hell, he saw enough as it was.

He looked the way he felt—like a two-bit, no-account loser who'd gotten himself scraped up again and was about to take to the road once more. Except that the grimness around his mouth seemed more intense. The shadows in his eyes were darker. He hadn't looked this defeated, this lost, since... since Jill. The difference was he'd been glad to make tracks and leave her behind in his dust. Maybe it had taken him some time to heal the wounds she'd caused, but he'd succeeded. This time wasn't going to be as easy.

He loved her. Rain Neelson...ex-virgin...member of the walking wounded club...a regular thorn in his side...his lover...his love... Couldn't she see it? Couldn't she tell?

He'd done everything but act like a damned puppy, following her every step since the day he'd arrived in this tick-size town. At first he'd tried to tell himself that he enjoyed riling her because she was an anomaly compared to the women he'd known. It was still true, in a way; but it was also true that from the first day he'd felt something for her, only he'd been fighting it.

How like him to fall for a decent woman, a good woman, the kind of woman a man built a future around. Guess he hadn't wandered too far from the fold after all. His mother would be proud—had he managed to make things work out. But what possessed him to think Rain could want anything more from someone like him than a few hours of novelty?

Good sex wasn't enough to build on. She'd made that clear after their first time together. As he felt a pinch in his shoulder and massaged around the bandage, he told himself he'd been a fool to think anything had changed. He should just be grateful for whatever it was that had brought her over here.

Now what? It was so quiet out there. Was she dressing, anxious to get away? He found her conflicting personality amusing. Endearing. She could block out her thoughts and focus entirely, honestly, on her sexuality. But once the tide of passion receded, there was no escaping that puritan mind of hers.

No doubt she was already tormented with guilt. He should make it easy for her, give her adequate time to make her quiet escape. Or he could go out there and say something that would make a clean break. Sweet heaven, he didn't think he could bear a drawn out goodbye.

But then he thought of how it had felt to have her hands on him, to be buried deep within her hot, tight little body. He fought back a moan as his body betrayed his mind.

Angry with himself and with the fate that had brought him to this place, he pounded his hand against the sink. The wrong hand.

"Jake!"

Even above the harsh curse he growled, he heard her concerned cry. Before the nuclear explosions stopped going off in front of his eyes and the nausea receded, she was cupping his throbbing hand with both of hers. He gave himself a shake and tried for a casual tone. "It's okay. I accidentally struck the sink, that's all."

Then he noticed she wasn't dressed. Hadn't even started. It was all he could focus on. She looked like a sleek little mermaid staring up at him, and he thought her eyes had never been so wide or sea blue. He discovered it hurt to look at her, even while desire came back with a vengeance, it hurt.

"You have to be more careful, Jake," she scolded gently.

"I know." And in the future he would be . . . about a lot of things, but mostly about letting quiet, gentle-faced women get under his skin and into his heart. "You okay?"

"I...yes."

"It was kinda quiet out there."

"Oh. Well, it's still raining and I thought... Did you want me to leave?"

He didn't answer. He couldn't. When she'd mentioned the rain, she'd reached up with both hands to touch her slicked back hair—as though he'd needed a reminder. He hadn't, just as he hadn't needed an excuse to admire her pretty breasts and the way her graceful movement lifted them in invitation.

He couldn't resist. He cupped her in his hands and brushed his thumbs across the twin, rosy peaks tempting him.

"Jake!"

He loved hearing the yearning in her voice, loved the way she automatically responded by swaying toward him. With a groan, he bent and replaced one of his thumbs with his mouth.

"Jake."

His body, having grown aroused the moment she'd come to him, betrayed him even more. Between its demands and the sweet seduction of her voice, he had no choice. Acting on reflex alone, he slipped his arms around her and set her on the sink.

"What are you...?"

"Don't say no." He parted her legs and showed her how to wrap them around his waist. "Don't...oh, jeez, don't say no."

It felt better than before. He didn't think it was possible, but it did. She accepted him so smoothly, he thought he would explode right there and then. When she wrapped her arms around his neck and intermittently spread kisses over his face while whispering his name, he thought it again. The instant he felt her lose control, go rigid against him, he knew it was all over. Feeling her pulsing around him, he buried his face in the warm curve of her neck and poured into her.

They shared a shower afterward. Neither of them seemed in the mood to talk and when she slipped out, he didn't try to stop her because it became impossible not to be around her without having his body embarrass him.

Not sure what he would find when he emerged, he exited the stall and took his time drying himself off. This time she would be gone, he told himself. Maybe she'd responded to him a second time, but by now she must have figured out what a selfish bastard he was and have the sense to get away.

Sure he was a glutton for punishment, but unable to withstand his curiosity any longer, he went to the doorway... and saw her waiting for him. She sat on his bed with the sheet wrapped around her. Gazing off into space, she looked young, vulnerable.

Jake crossed over to her. Unwilling to deny himself the luxury, he stood still as she took his injured hand and inspected it herself.

"Maybe you should wear a glove while you're driving so you won't cause too much abrasion," she said, her voice as quiet as her concentration was intense. "A leather one. Do you have something like that?"

"Yeah. Somewhere. I'll try it."

"Good, because... a burn that gets infected can be as serious as... anything."

"I'd heard that. I'll, er, be careful."

She released him and, because it was unignorable, dealt with the reality of his being aroused again. Slowly, so slowly he thought he wouldn't be able to bear it, she reached out and gently touched him. His breath left him in a tortured rush.

"I never thought a man could be so smooth and soft."

He didn't feel very soft. In fact if she continued her feather-light touch much longer, he was afraid of what could happen. When she caressed him with her cheek, it was too much.

He took hold of her head and lifted it to receive his desperate kiss. As before, like the first time, Rain reacted with a stunning, gratifying honesty. She rose to her knees and wrapped her arms around his waist, matching his passion as no one before ever had, and he knew never would again.

"Stay with me." He dragged her higher, needing to have more of her against him.

"Yes."

"Stay the night."

"I—"

"The night, Rain."

"All right."

Like a fever their passion soared. Too fast. Not fast enough. By the time Jake lowered her to the already damp sheets, he felt the new dampness that moistened their bodies. Both of their bodies. It pleased him that she wasn't totally able to rationalize and seemed as caught up in this as he was, and as helpless to hide it. If he could have nothing else, he would take this memory with him. Rain...outside...inside...surrounding him, cleansing his weary, damaged heart.

A gift.

But one he couldn't keep.

The cot was too short and narrow for both of them to have fallen asleep, but the next thing Rain knew it was dark. Only the glow of the security lights filtering through a crack in a curtain here and there illuminated the trailer.

She lay on her side with Jake wrapped around her like a shell on a turtle. It should have been unbearable considering the rain had left its usual blanket of humidity thickening the air and making any contact stifling. Plus she wasn't used to sleeping with anyone.

Nevertheless, she'd slept as one who hadn't a care in the world, a state so far from reality that she had to fight back an abrupt, bitter laugh. Her sudden tension had Jake drawing in a deep breath and tightening his arms.

He was listening, gauging, she thought, noting his stillness. Thinking what? Was he regretting having asked her to stay?

"Okay?"

His gruff whisper held sweet concern. She hated that her throat locked with emotion. "Mmm."

"I'm too heavy for you."

"No, it's only hot and I was thinking about getting something to drink." Be careful, she warned herself. If he saw too much, it would only ruin these last precious hours.

"I'm sorry, but I think there's only beer in the refrigerator."

She'd never cared for beer; however, if it was cold and wet, she would make allowances. Jake was closest to the wall, so by virtue of positioning, she went to get it. It didn't bother her, until she opened the refrigerator door and was illuminated by the inside light. She'd forgotten about that.

His gaze was a physical thing, reminding her of the honest intensity they'd been sharing. Once again it made her wish she was more voluptuous and attractive. Pure foolishness, all things considered. Why couldn't she be grateful that he'd been able to give her this much? she thought sternly, returning and sitting down beside him.

She flipped open the tab and took a needful sip. "Ugh," she sputtered, grimacing.

"It's an acquired taste." He took the can from her and downed a third of the can before handing it back to her. "Try another."

There was no way she would ever grow to like the stuff, but she had to admit the second sip wasn't as bad. At least it helped ease the sandpapery feeling in her throat and her feverishness. She found a better use for the can by rubbing it across her forehead. "This is the first time in my life I've ever considered what it would be like to live in a cooler climate."

"Like where?"

"As steamy as it is, I'm picturing way up. Northern Alaska?"

"You'd have to put more meat on your bones to survive," he drawled. "Though, it would be interesting to watch an Eskimo's reaction to your drawl."

"That's rich coming from a Texan." Actually Jake didn't have a heavy accent. She couldn't pick it up at all unless he deliberately teased or tried to annoy her. Had his travels done that? Did you really lose yourself, your "ear" if you traveled as much as he did?

"Why do you do that?"

"Do what?"

"Carry on a conversation without me. It's something I noticed about you from the beginning. You don't ask questions. You don't make observations. I know you're bright, which means you're inquisitive, and yet you've never really asked me anything, except when you felt a need to fill what you've decided is an awkward silence."

It struck her as strange that someone would chide her for having good manners. "My mother raised me to believe it was impolite to poke my nose in someone else's personal business."

"We're talking about making conversation, not rehashing the Inquisition. I don't get it," he said, his tone wry. "I mean, I am the man you've just made love with."

Made love with. Did he really think of it in those terms? Was it more than sex to him? Anyone else would probably think her an oversensitive idiot for picking up on the word, but it meant a great deal to her.

"Old habits die hard," she murmured, turning the can because she knew she couldn't swallow right now to save her life. When she realized how obvious the gesture was, she offered the beer to him. "Go ahead, finish it. I'm fine now."

But she wasn't fine. As he drank she watched the headlights of a passing car illuminate the fake-wood paneling, thinking about the innumerable things she did want to know about him. Like what made him happy? What frightened him? When was the last time he wept? What were his biggest regrets? Did he see himself settling down someday, maybe even having a family? Where would he go once he left Stiles? What would he say if she asked him to take her with him?

The last thought shocked her. There was no way, of course, that she could be comfortable with the rootless life he seemed to prefer. Her entire history was here. On holidays she still went to the cemetery on the other side of town to visit her parents' grave. Even though she might well die an old maid, it made her feel less lonely to know that every day of the week there was someplace she was expected to be. People counted on her presence. She *needed* to feel needed, even if it was only to unlock a safe and authorize a money order so someone could pay a speeding ticket in another county or send an expectant grandchild a birthday gift. Not everyone had been born for a life of adventure.

"Don't block me out."

She realized he was watching her. His expression was hard to define in the darkness, but what light there was made his eyes glow with an inner fire she preferred to pretend—at least in the privacy of her heart—was longing.

"I was thinking about the woman you..." She couldn't make herself say it and altered the words to, "Your brother's wife."

"Jill. I guessed it might be something like that. What do you want to know?"

How about everything? She reached for laughter and had to settle for a shrug. "Nothing. I was thinking about her, that's all."

He made a *tsking* sound, and set the beer on the side table. "Worse than pulling teeth."

"Oh, all right," Rain muttered. "Was she beautiful?"

Jake took her hand and began lacing and unlacing her fingers with his. "Outwardly... yeah. In the looks department she was an angel. Tall, blond and built in a way to make a man forget what day of the week it was. Inside," he continued with a sigh, "she was empty. Except for greed. She did have that—or does, I should say. But not much else. Believe me, she and Jack are well suited for each other. The only difference is that unlike their nursery rhyme counterparts they haven't 'tumbled' yet."

Rain found she was too human. Instead of taking heart from the fact that Jake thought Jill was cruel and selfish, all she could dwell on was that the woman was lovely. How could someone like *her* compete?

"Do you know what I thought when I first saw you?"

Despite her melancholy state of mind, she managed a brief smile. "No, and I'm not sure I want to."

"Yes, you do. Your honesty and realness struck me right between the eyes. 'There was a woman,' I told myself, 'who wasn't a stranger to her own body or desires.'"

"Guess I proved you wrong," Rain muttered, wishing she could wipe that horrible day from her memory.

"Uh-uh." Jake rose on an elbow. "Okay, so you were embarrassed when you realized I was watching. The point is that when you decided you were ready to take on a lover, it was *your* decision. Honey, to a guy who's spent most of his adult life trying to figure out why he doesn't fit in anywhere that was a mighty big bite of humble pie to swallow."

"You?"

"Me." He offered a reassuring smile. "This might be a small town, but small towns magnify everything. You probably never thought of running away. You've made a place for yourself here, and on your terms."

She didn't think she had, not well at all. Agreed, maybe she hadn't run as he had, but she'd wasted too much time wishing she was something else.

"Go on," Jake prompted. "What else?"

Rain felt her thoughts jerked back to the present. "Pardon?"

"Ask me something else. Anything. We've been as close as two people can be. Tomorrow I'm going to climb on that metal mustang out there, probably point it in the direction of the prevailing wind and follow the road to wherever. I don't know when or if I'll ever get back this way again," he added, although Rain could have done without hearing that. "Isn't there something you've always wanted to know about me?"

Yes, she cried silently, thinking him almost cruel to constantly remind her. *Tell me what you feel when you're inside me? How can you think of leaving when my heart's breaking? What would you say if I told you I didn't mean to complicate this with love, but I have?*

She gazed at him sadly. "Sometimes it's best not to ask for too much . . . or to hold on to memories too tightly."

"I see. You plan to forget me as soon as I'm gone?"

Before she could reply, he sat up and framed her face with his hands. "Ask me about my favorite song."

Maybe he'd suffered a concussion in the fall he'd had yesterday. "I don't understand?"

"It's 'One More Night.'"

"I'm not familiar with it."

"Look it up sometime."

"Yes, of course. I didn't even know you like music."

"Mostly R and B, some country and an occasional dose of gospel. I also prefer fried chicken over beef," he continued, pushing her back onto the bed, "beer over bourbon, and I do all my deep thinking in a shower."

"Speaking of showers," she mumbled, convinced something really was wrong with him, "it's stopped raining."

"Who cares?"

"No, I thought . . . we said before . . ." She couldn't bring herself to say it. "It's terribly hot. I think I'll go rinse off."

But the instant she tried to slip off the bed, he pulled her back and covered her with his body. "Don't. Don't wash me, my touch off you," he ground out. "Not yet. Not until you have to."

"I didn't mean . . ." Rain touched his still-damp hair, his feverish skin, his bandaged shoulder. She held him close when he came completely into her arms. "Oh, Jake. How do you do this to me?"

Sometimes he broke her heart. It was when he became like this—so much vulnerability in a man's body—that he threatened to destroy her. Couldn't he see she was no better equipped for what was happening, no stronger than he was?

Just say it, Jake. Tell me what I need to hear and we'll work things out somehow.

"Hold me," he demanded.

"Yes."

"Kiss me."

She did.

"Ask me for something. Anything. Damn it, tell me what you want," he muttered, spreading hot kisses over her face until her breaths grew as shallow as his. "I haven't given you anything. Ask me for something!"

"Love me . . . I mean once more. Make love to me one last time."

"Damn it, Rain," he groaned. "Damn *you*."

She didn't understand his anger, but she welcomed his passion. His fierce kiss was punishing and yet desperate. Rain couldn't have resisted it if she'd wanted to.

As he pressed her deep into the bed, she held him fast. When he molded his mouth to hers, she buried her hands in his hair and matched him kiss for kiss. The subsequent journey of his hands over her already heated body was no less determined and intense than hers.

But when he started to taste her body as though she were a lush dessert, a heady aperitif, she began to doubt her ability to keep her secret to herself. Never had her breasts been so sensitive to his touch. Never had his hands, his lips, moved with such skill. He left no inch of her unexplored, until her body hummed with long suppressed needs that left her trembling.

When he reached the flat plain of her belly, she began to wonder if she could bear it. When his hands and then his mouth explored lower, she bit her lip to hold back a whimper. And when he gently but firmly parted her thighs and did things she'd never truly believed was part of what went on between lovers outside a novel, she gripped his shoulders and hair and begged him to stop, to help her, to come inside her.

Then he was there, holding her as she held him, their bodies slick and straining. And still she felt in him a driving need for more.

They reached the pinnacle at the same instant she thought she had nothing left to give. He captured her cry with his mouth and his answering groan rumbled like distant thunder after the most devastating of storms.

When peace came, and it did so ever so slowly, it felt heavy and incredibly sad. Rain knew in her heart that now they had come to their end. It was why she resisted letting go, and why she refused to succumb to sleep despite her body's exhaustion.

But Jake slept. Within moments his even breathing told her that little could rouse him now. She didn't mind. It gave her the privacy she needed to let her long-contained tears flow. They poured like a flooding river over a crumbling dam. Only because her pillow was already damp from her wet hair, she barely noticed.

Ten

It took Jake a considerable while to rise out of his deep sleep. The instant he knew he was alone, his contentment and heartfelt joy vanished.

Cautious, still hopeful, he rose on an elbow. "Rain?"

Of course there was no answer. He knew better than to expect one. And yet for an instant he'd thought... That last time they'd made love, she'd been with him all the way. How could she have walked out?

But her clothes were gone and there was nothing left to prove she'd been here except the empty beer can and her damp pillow... and his memories. He frowned as he ran his hand over the pillow. This had been what finally woke him. He'd pulled it close in his sleep, thinking it was her. His hair had been wet, too, but his pillow had almost dried. Admittedly, hers was longer, still...

He swore and sat up. What had he done to make her cry? How could she leave him after what they'd shared?

Work, you fool. She had to go to work.

He glanced at the clock and almost exhaled a long sigh of relief. Then the white slip of paper on the kitchen table drew his attention. A smile tugged at his lips as, naked, he pushed himself to his feet and went to read it.

No one had ever left him a note before. It made him feel special, as though he belonged. Needed, there was the best part. She did need him. He squinted to read it in the early gray of first daylight.

Please don't say goodbye. Just go.

The scrap of paper slipped from his hands. Whether it was the words or her shaky scrawl that got to him didn't matter, but he felt a pain that nearly bent him from the waist. She might as well have used a knife on him. As it was, he could almost feel his blood pouring out of his invisible wound.

"Damn it!" he ground out. She was going to do it. She wanted to throw them, what they'd shared, away like so much trash? He thought he'd finally come to know her; how could he be so wrong about someone twice in his life? All these years, he thought darkly, hadn't he learned anything? Swearing again, he stalked to the bathroom.

Every few minutes Rain glanced up at the clock. Not because she had to unlock the front door soon for business, but because she was estimating how long it had probably been since Jake had awakened. And found her message. That was what really put her nerves to the test: how would he take the note she'd left him?

She'd debated not leaving anything. But then he would likely have called her, stopped by. The mere thought of him walking in here and forcing her to deal with her heartbreak in front of everyone was enough to make her empty stomach queasy.

He would be showered now and finished packing.
Would he have stayed, waiting for Angus? Visited for a
while? She couldn't see that he would be in a mood for
small talk this morning, at least she hoped he wasn't. She
hoped he would miss her. Please let him miss her. Some.

Would he take the road leading to the highway or ignore her note, drive by and wave? She could probably
deal with that. It would be nice to have a mental picture
to remember him by.

Liar.

Yes, she was a liar. She didn't want a memory, she
wanted *him*. She wanted him to walk through that door
and tell her that he'd changed his mind and had decided
to stay on awhile longer. It didn't matter if it would only
be delaying the inevitable. It would be worth it. There
would be time to store up more memories. And given
time, who knew? He might even change his mind. He
could conceivably learn to love her as much as she loved
him.

"It's time."

She looked up from the blur of paperwork before her
and saw George had joined her at the counter. He was
watching her, but not unkindly.

With a nod, she reached for her keys. At least they
seemed to have resolved their problem, she thought with
an inner sigh. Considering how things could have turned
out, she should be more grateful. But it was difficult to
feel anything beneath her numbed state other than the
dull ache of loss. Which, she added ruefully, would surely
turn into a full-fledged pain once she knew for certain
that he'd gone.

"Let me do it. Are you sure you're all right? I don't
mean to keep harping on it, but you're awfully pale this
morning."

Rain struggled for a wry smile. "I guess I didn't get all the sleep I needed last night."

"Yeah, that was a good rain, wasn't it?"

"The best."

"As I was driving in, it was all they spoke about on the radio farm program."

"Guess the farmers are indulging in a collective sigh of relief," Rain replied, amazed she could manage such bland prattle when inside she felt she might be dying.

Despite having passed over the keys, George lingered. When she finally realized he was shifting uncomfortably, she lifted an eyebrow in inquiry.

"I wanted to say... What I mean is, if you're not feeling well, and you'd like to take off, I'd... well, I owe you."

"Thanks, George," she replied sincerely. "I can't tell you how touched I am that you made the gesture. But work is probably the best thing for me."

At least she thought it was, until George opened the shades on the glass door and partition and she saw who their first customer of the day would be. She groaned inwardly. There was no way she was ready to deal with him yet.

The moment George unlocked the door and began pulling it open, he squeezed inside. "Good morning, Gil," she murmured, intent on keeping her tone polite. She was glad, however, that she'd remained behind the counter. Maybe her trembling wouldn't show as much.

"Where were you last night?" he demanded, the instant he reached the counter.

His glare was so preposterous, so accusing, it took her a moment to think of a reply. "Excuse me?"

"I phoned your house last night. You weren't there."

Although she could feel the heat of embarrassment rise to her cheeks because she knew George was still in hearing distance, Rain was furious. "You have no business talking to me that way, Gil, just as you had no business checking on me. As a result, I have no intention of answering you."

"You were with him, weren't you?"

Rain matched him glare for glare. How dare he embarrass her in front of her staff, and where did he get off with this sudden possessiveness? When she began to turn away, having decided to ask George to escort him out, he reached across the counter and grabbed her wrist.

"Get your hands off my woman, Wakefield."

Rain gasped. Gil spun around. George and Malva... oh, God, Rain moaned, noticing everyone had come up front, would she ever have anything significant happen to her in this town that didn't become a community event?

Like her, they all stared at the man in the black T-shirt and jeans filling the doorway like some cinema antihero. Gil recovered first. He turned his back on Jake and stared at her as though seeing her for the first time. No, she amended, as though she'd sprouted serpents from her hair or something equally repelling.

"You had to have your revenge, didn't you?" he muttered accusingly.

"Have you lost your mind? You're married, Gil. What I do or don't do is none of your business."

"Of all the men you could have chosen, did you have to insult me by reducing yourself to *him?*"

He never got to say more. In two strides Jake had him by the scruff of the neck. "Let's take a little walk, Wakefield," he growled, and hustled him back out the door.

Everyone watched as Jake half dragged, half carried him through the lobby and then out of the building. Through the front plate-glass windows they saw him send Gil sprawling across the patch of green grass and into the red-and-white circle of petunias framing the flagpole. To her dismay, even as Gil's knees slid across the lawn, traffic stopped on the road, people came to the window of the café. And next door at the barber shop, Chief of Police Ed Rogers appeared on the sidewalk, still draped with a protective sheet.

"Good riddance," Malva said, breaking the stark silence.

All Rain could do was stare at the chief and pray he didn't arrest Jake. Already Gil was protesting to him and pointing wildly at Jake. She nearly wept with relief when Ed simply threw back his head, laughed and walked back into the barber shop.

Jake took his time returning. He walked up to the counter with a definite swagger, Rain thought warily. If it wasn't for the way he was flexing his burned hand, she might have been truly worried.

"Did you hurt it again?" she asked, itching to reach out and soothe.

"Forget the hand." He stopped directly in front of her and stared across the counter. "What the hell is going on?"

His voice was hard and his look was bitter. Rain gestured to where Gil was finally brushing himself off and walking away in disgust. "I don't know what got into him. I certainly didn't encourage him, Jake."

"I know."

"You do?" She managed a hopeful smile. "I thought . . . I assumed you'd be gone by now."

"Assumed or hoped?"

Her smile withered. He was angry, and at her. Why?

"Why'd you run away this morning?"

"I didn't run," she replied, her heart pounding in her throat. "I—"

"Ran."

"Jake, I had to come to work." She cast a fleeting look toward her crew and saw they hadn't budged.

"So you decided to leave me a note telling me to haul my butt out of town without even bothering to say goodbye?"

"That's not what it meant and you know it."

"Why, Rain? Were you embarrassed someone would know we were lovers?"

"Jake!" This time she noticed the considerable crowd they were collecting in the lobby. Several hands were helping to keep the door open so their conversation could be heard and everyone was wide-eyed with fascination. "I don't think this is either the time or the place," she said, feeling the heat of a mortified blush sting her face.

"Hell, when is it a good time? You never *talk* to me!"

"Look who's complaining—Mr. My-Life's-An-Open-Book himself!"

They glared at each other for several breath-holding seconds. Rain heard someone in the lobby whisper, "What are they saying now? I can't hear a thing."

"That's because they're at a stalemate," someone else whispered back.

"Answer one question," Jake said, his voice so low it almost sounded like a growl. "Do you love me?"

"You have to ask that? Isn't it obvious?"

"Yes!" he roared back. "I have to ask, and no, it isn't obvious. Damn it, that's the problem!"

The windows shook. Taken aback, Rain could only wonder what he was trying to do to her. When he reached out his hand, she shook her head, unwilling to expose herself any further without some reassurance.

"Come here, Rain. We have to talk."

"I am not saying another word. Look at all these people!"

He didn't take his eyes off her, nor did he withdraw his hand. "Jump up, honey. I'll lift you over."

She knew she'd lost her mind when she found herself glancing again at George and Malva. Seeing both of them grinning was no help whatsoever.

"Go for it," Malva told her.

"Go ahead," George echoed. "We'll manage."

"But Norm is still on vacation and—"

"I told you I owe you," George replied. "Give me a chance to start paying you back."

Nearly drawing blood as she again bit at her lip, she looked back at Jake, letting him see the uncertainty and fear in her eyes. His answering expression of intense reassurance gave her the courage to snatch up her purse from under the counter and boost herself up onto the counter. Then Jake's strong hands gripped her waist and he swept her into his arms.

Somebody whistled, someone else—she thought it was Malva—hooted.

"Jake, you can put me down now."

"Not until I have you safely where you won't run off on me again."

He was as good as his word. Carrying her outside, he set her on his motorcycle and, followed by cheers and waves, drove them the short distance to her house. Having never been on a motorcycle before, Rain found the whole experience a bit intimidating—when she wasn't trying to wrestle the wind and keep her skirt down.

At her house, he took hold of her wrist and led her inside. Rain found it difficult to ignore Angus's howling laughter and protested the entire way.

The moment he slammed the front door behind them, she declared, "Have you lost your—"

He crushed his mouth to hers, cutting her short. His tongue drove deep, destroying her will as easily, as completely, as he had claimed her body mere hours ago. Within seconds he had her clinging weakly to him, answering his hot kisses with her own.

His hands moved over her as though he couldn't touch her enough. And then the words came, "I love you. Oh, God, I love you," bringing tears to her eyes and joy to her heart.

She framed his face with her hands. "Is it true?"

"I've never said anything I mean more."

"Why didn't you tell me?"

"I was fighting it. I thought all you wanted was a quick fling, to get back at Wakefield."

"I thought I did," she admitted, ashamed of herself for ever considering the idea. "Until you showed me how wrong I was."

"Did I?" he asked softly.

The sweet desperation in his expression made Rain's heart overflow with emotion. She'd thought him bad? A dangerous man? She'd been wrong. He was every bit as sexually breathtaking as she'd guessed, but he was also her heart and her life. "Yes. Oh, I love you, too, Jake."

"Prove it," he said with the same daring look he'd used that afternoon weeks ago.

It reminded Rain of how blind she'd been and how she'd misjudged him. He'd wanted her, truly wanted her then, too. With a renewed surge of joy, she took his hand and led him to her bedroom. Once there she dragged his

T-shirt up from the waistband of his jeans and over his head, careful not to brush against his bandaged shoulder. Flinging it away, she ran her hands over his hot chest, thrilling to the knowledge that she could make his heart beat so strongly, his pulse race this frantically. When she touched her parted mouth to his left nipple, he groaned and buried his hands in her hair.

"How could I leave this?" he rasped as she continued to kiss him while unbuckling his belt. "How could I walk away from you? Do you think I could ever touch another woman again and not compare her with the way you look at me, come to me...want me?"

Somehow, despite her trembling hands, she managed to get his pants open, and slid her hand under the elastic waistband of his briefs. His breath caught and he pressed himself into her hand. Once. Twice. But with a groan, he made her stop, and carefully but urgently, coaxed her down on the bed.

Rain's heart overflowed with new joy when she noticed his own hands were shaking. Soon, however, he'd wrestled with her clothes just enough to make a place for himself and she focused on nothing except their merging.

"Do you know what I thought of when I read your note? That last night, after the first time, I'd lost my head and hadn't protected you. Here you were ready to say goodbye, and you could already be pregnant with our child."

"I didn't think about that," Rain admitted, a warm glow filling her as she did now.

"I couldn't stop. In fact I liked the idea so much I decided I'm not letting anything come between us again," he said, drawing a gasp from her as he slid deeply into her yielding body.

Never had he filled her more completely. "Never again," she agreed. "Oh, Jake, I want you so much."

"Tell me. Say what I've been waiting to hear."

"I love you," she whispered, the pleasure almost unbearable.

Jake laced his fingers with hers. "Again."

"I love you."

"Enough to marry me?"

Her gaze was adoring. "Yes. But are you sure?"

His thrusts became more intense and with them his voice. "I need you, sweetheart. We need each other."

It was the last time either of them spoke for several minutes. It was all that needed to be said for passion to take control. Holding each other tightly, they raced for the bliss that had been their guiding beacon all along.

A long while afterward, Jake lifted his head and brushed a tender kiss across Rain's lips, her chin, her nose. "Still upset with me for kidnapping you?"

"I should be, but I can't seem to summon the energy."

"Maybe you should take the rest of the day off and recuperate."

She laughed softly, but shook her head. "As much as I'd love to, I can't take advantage like that."

"Something tells me that your cohorts would be disappointed if you showed up any sooner than tomorrow. Besides, we could also use the time to get our blood tests and marriage license."

She couldn't believe what she was hearing. It was one thing to dream, quite another to have her fantasies become part of reality. "This is happening so fast, Jake. Are you sure? We haven't known each other very long."

"Don't compare what we have to your experience with Wakefield, honey. Maybe we don't have the numbers time wise to prove it, but can you tell me that fate didn't somehow mean for us to find each other?"

"I'd like to believe that, and I do," she assured him. "Until I think of how different we are."

"Are we really?" He raised an eyebrow, which gave him a devilish look. "You think I'm irreverent and—was it 'bad' you called me? Well, honey, the way you came on to me that day we first made love...you were badder than bad."

She knew she turned scarlet. "Don't remind me. Sometimes I still can't believe I was that brazen."

"I wouldn't have you any other way," he replied, reassuring her with a kiss. "And as time goes on, I'm confident we'll learn lots of other things we have in common." Suddenly he grew more serious. "We were two lonely people looking for someone to love us for ourselves, sweetheart. I think we've accomplished that, don't you?"

She told him she did, but she had one more worry. "This is a small town, Jake. Are you sure you won't get bored?"

"I'll be too busy across the street."

She'd forgotten all about his having to worry about employment. In a small town that was more than a passing concern. "Your job was supposed to be temporary. Are you sure Angus will keep you on?"

"I doubt it. That's why I spoke to him before I came to you and offered to buy him out."

"You did!"

"Well, I knew I couldn't stay if I didn't have a way to earn a living, and the last thing I wanted to do was have to ask you to relocate."

"But I would, if you wanted me to."

"I know." His smile was as loving as it was grateful, and he kissed her again. "That's part of what got to me about you from the beginning. You stand by those you love no matter what. I wanted that faith and dedication for myself. I guess I've always been searching for it."

"And you really want to buy the garage?"

"Why not? Angus has developed a solid clientele, and I've got a nice nest egg saved up since I've never spent much during the years I've been on the road. I'm also handier with cars than he is. What's more, I have plenty of ideas on how to fix up the place."

"I'll help!" Rain promised with a rueful look. "I've been wanting to get my hands on that eyesore for ages."

Jake rolled onto his back, carrying her with him. His dark eyes twinkled with mischief. "Great . . . as long as your priority is to keep your hands on *me*."

"I promise," she whispered.

Long, sweet moments later a distant rumble caught their attention.

Rain lifted her head. "Was that what I think it was?"

Jake grinned. "It appears everyone's drought is over."

Catching on to his innuendo, Rain touched a finger to his lips. "You're bad, Jake Marlowe."

He slid his hands to her bottom and began rocking her slowly against him. "Yeah . . . and you're my inspiration. Ah, God, Rain . . . love me."

"With all my heart," she whispered, lowering her mouth to his. "And for always."

*   *   *   *   *

Fifty red-blooded, white-hot, true-blue hunks from every State in the Union!

Beginning in May, look for MEN MADE IN AMERICA! Written by some of our most popular authors, these stories feature fifty of the strongest, sexiest men, each from a different state in the union!

Two titles available every other month at your favorite retail outlet.

In July, look for:

CALL IT DESTINY by Jayne Ann Krentz (Arizona)
ANOTHER KIND OF LOVE by Mary Lynn Baxter (Arkansas)

In September, look for:

DECEPTIONS by Annette Broadrick (California)
STORMWALKER by Dallas Schulze (Colorado)

You won't be able to resist MEN MADE IN AMERICA!

Relive the romance...
Harlequin and Silhouette
are proud to present

by Request

A program of collections of three complete novels by the most requested authors with the most requested themes. Be sure to look for one volume each month with three complete novels by top name authors.

In June: **NINE MONTHS** Penny Jordan
Stella Cameron
Janice Kaiser

Three women pregnant and alone. But a lot can happen in nine months!

In July: **DADDY'S HOME** Kristin James
Naomi Horton
Mary Lynn Baxter

Daddy's Home ... and his presence is long overdue!

In August: **FORGOTTEN PAST** Barbara Kaye
Pamela Browning
Nancy Martin

Do you dare to create a future if you've forgotten the past?

Available at your favorite retail outlet.

Silhouette Books
is proud to present
our best authors,
their best books...
and the best in
your reading pleasure!

Throughout 1993, look for exciting
books by these top names in
contemporary romance:

DIANA PALMER—
Fire and Ice in June

ELIZABETH LOWELL—
Fever in July

CATHERINE COULTER—
Afterglow in August

LINDA HOWARD—
Come Lie With Me in September

When it comes to passion,
we wrote the book.

BOBT2

If you've been looking for something a little bit different and a little bit spooky, let Silhouette Books take you on a journey to the dark side of love with

Every month, Silhouette will bring you two romantic, spine-tingling Shadows novels, written by some of your favorite authors, such as *New York Times* bestselling author Heather Graham Pozzessere, Anne Stuart, Helen R. Myers and Rachel Lee—to name just a few.

In July, look for:
HEART OF THE BEAST by Carla Cassidy
DARK ENCHANTMENT by Jane Toombs

In August, look for:
A SILENCE OF DREAMS by Barbara Faith
THE SEVENTH NIGHT by Amanda Stevens

In September, look for:
FOOTSTEPS IN THE NIGHT by Lee Karr
WHAT WAITS BELOW by Jane Toombs

*Come into the world of Shadows and prepare
to tremble with fear—and passion....*

SILHOUETTE® Desire®

RED, WHITE AND BLUE...
Six sexy, hardworking, hometown hunks who were born and bred in the USA!

NEED PROTECTION?
Then you must read ZEKE #793 by Annette Broadrick
July's Man of the Month

NEED TO TAKE THE PLUNGE?
Then dive into BEN #794 by Karen Leabo

NEED TO GET AWAY?
Then sail away with DEREK #795 by Leslie Davis Guccione

NEED TO FIND YOUR ROOTS?
Then dig into CAMERON #796 by Beverly Barton

NEED A MAN?
Then warm up with JAKE #797 by Helen R. Myers

NEED A HAND?
Then you need to meet WILL #798 by Kelly Jamison

Desire invites you to meet these sexy, down-home guys! These hunks are HOT and will make you pledge allegiance to the all-American man!

SDRWB